Books by Somtow Sucharitkul

THE FALLEN COUNTRY

science fiction and fantasy:

STARSHIP & HAIKU
MALLWORLD
THE INQUESTOR TETRALOGY
THE AQUILIAD
FIRE FROM THE WINE-DARK SEA
THE ALIEN SWORDMASTER

as S. P. Somtow:

VAMPIRE JUNCTION
THE SHATTERED HORSE
FORGETTING PLACES

S.P. SOMTOW
FORGETTING PLACES

TOR

for Matthew Tabery

I wish you were still here.

FORGETTING PLACES

Copyright © 1987 by S. P. Somtow

First printing: October 1987

A TOR Book

Published by Tom Doherty Associates, Inc.
49 West 24 Street
New York, N.Y. 10010

ISBN: 0-312-93030-5

Library of Congress Catalog Card Number: 87-50475

Printed in the United States of America

0 9 8 7 6 5 4 3 2 1

Contents

CHAPTER 1

If I Can't Remember It, It Can't Be True

MY BROTHER HAD the bad luck to be born in the early seventies. That's why he was named Benjamin Bhakti Madigan. Acquaintances called him B.B. for short. But I always called him Ben, and I always will. "Bhakti" is some kind of Oriental philosophy thing —my parents used to be hippies, though today you would never guess. Before I was born, they came to McDougal, Kansas, which is just a stone's throw from Colorado beside the Arkansas River, in order to "find" themselves. McDougal is a beautiful, picture-postcard kind of place, and there is a ghost town nearby that tourists sometimes get to. It is also stunningly dull. There used to be a commune here, but most everyone went back to the real world long ago. They're all computer scientists or real estate brokers or something else respectable. My parents aimed at respectability too, but they didn't quite make it—they own a small bookstore in a mall about twenty miles down Route 50. *Almost* respectable. I think they started calling my brother B.B. because they were kind of embarrassed to have named him after something they'd heard in a guru self-awareness encounter session.

As for me, they call me J.J. It doesn't stand for

1

anything. Well, maybe it does, but I haven't told anyone since first grade, and I'm not going to now.

No two people could have been more different from each other than me and my big brother. I have always been a standard-issue kind of kid. That year, my freshman year at McDougal High, I did video games, baseball, shopping malls, new wave music, and bad horror movies. My brother was more of a genius. He read a lot of books. He also wrote things, but he rarely showed them to anyone. And he used to build things in the basement—you know, robots from erector sets, spaceships from junk. He knew about werewolves, witches, and weird religions. If you weren't feeling charitable, you might have called him a nerd. But I wanted to be exactly like him. Maybe if I tried hard enough, I would be. I would copy the way he dressed and talked, sometimes without even thinking. Sometimes he'd say to me, "Seems like whatever I do, you'll be doing the same thing by the next day." Maybe it annoyed him a little, but it was true and I didn't want it any other way. Then he went and killed himself.

For a long time, like a whole year maybe, I couldn't remember much about it. They told me I'd blanked it from my mind so I could deal with it better. But I knew how I'd found him, because I read it in the paper the next day. It said how I came upon him leaning against a tree in the woods between our backyard and the bank of the Arkansas River. How I didn't come home that night and they found me in the parking lot of Mr. Miles's general store, glassy-eyed and shivering. I was in a daze and I was covered in blood and I was no help to the police. At least they knew *I* didn't do it. That was something to do with the fingerprints on the gun, or the angle of the shot, something like that. I didn't even know we had a gun in the house.

The only thing I really remembered vividly was the mess—the blood. And the sour stench of fallen leaves, decaying, smeared with blood. And the wind, stirring the dead foliage, carrying the smell of the river. And thinking, "He expects me to do it too now. Because anything he does, I do."

I didn't cry or run screaming or anything like that. I don't remember feeling any pain, any grief. Nothing like that at all. I didn't have a name for the feelings I had, but I bottled them all up inside. For later. The whole world was waiting for me to crack and I wasn't going to give in.

After they brought me home, the doctor took a look at me, and then I went straight to the shower. I had missed Mr. Kavaldjian, the undertaker. The phone kept ringing.

I didn't say anything to my parents or my little sister. I just went to bed. I didn't toss and turn. Maybe it was from the pills the doctor gave me. They dulled the edge of my anger. But I was still determined not to give anything away.

I left the connecting door between my room and Ben's open, as I always did. When I woke up, I could see it was shut. My parents were in the room, talking in whispers so I wouldn't wake up.

I closed my eyes. They didn't notice and went on talking.

"How can he sleep? Doesn't he understand what's happened?" My mom's voice was strained. She'd probably been crying all night. "Could he really be that insensitive?"

"Now, Alice, don't panic. Dr. Geoghegan said it's perfectly normal for the kid to be into denial right now. Anyway, you'll wake him."

"They were so close. He must have known something, suspected something . . . *felt* something."

But that wasn't true. Were they still trying to pin it on me? It had to be a bad dream. I tried to remember the scene again, but my mind kept coming up blank. I thought: "If I can't remember it, it can't be true." I wanted them to stop talking about it, so I moved, pulled the blanket up over my eyes.

"Shh. He's awake," my father said.

I looked at the two of them. "Where's Ben?" I said. I didn't stop to think. My mother started to cry again. Her clothes were crumpled. She hadn't changed since yesterday. I thought, "Stop, please stop." Then I said, "I'm sorry."

"There's nothing to be sorry about," my father said. He hadn't shaved. Why did I get the feeling he didn't exactly mean it? "You don't have to go to school today if you don't want, son."

"I want to."

"We can't make him—" Mom began. "James—" she said, pulling at Dad's sleeve. The smell of burning bacon wafted upstairs. And the sound of my two-year-old sister crying. "God damn it!" my mother screamed. Then she stopped herself and looked at me in a funny kind of way. I knew she was upset because I wasn't hollering and carrying on the way I was supposed to.

"Maybe it's better," Dad said. "For him to go to school, I mean. Give him space, Alice." It was another of those hippie sayings. It sounded so false, coming from a balding man with a tweed jacket and a silly tie that advertised our bookstore. Dad couldn't look me in the eye. He glanced nervously outside my bedroom window with its *Return of the Jedi* draperies, and I heard people outside.

"For God's sake, tell them to leave, tell them to get out of here," Mom said, sobbing.

"I don't think they will," Dad said ruefully.

From behind Ben's closed door came the sound of our computer's speech synthesizer: "Time to wake up! Ta-da!"

When I went downstairs, I saw who they were: a mobile news unit from the local TV station. They'd been staking out the house all morning, waiting for one of us to emerge. I didn't eat breakfast, slipped out the back way, and detoured through the woods to where Ben and I used to catch the school bus.

The odor of death was gone. There wasn't any blood. They had cleaned it all away, and falling leaves had buried yesterday's sneaker prints. Just as though nothing had happened. I couldn't see the river, but the autumn wind was moist and powerful. I didn't linger. Even though the events had vanished from my mind, there was a hole down there waiting to be plugged. I hurried down to the side of the road, where the bus was just pulling in. I could hear the kids' voices, squabbling, chattering. As though today weren't any different from all the other days.

Wildly I thought, "It hasn't happened after all!" Again I struggled to pull the memory out of that dark hole . . . but all I found was the sickening smell . . . and a fleeting sight of blood.

If I can't remember it, it can't be true. . . .

As soon as the other kids saw me standing alone by the side of the road, the babble stopped. I got on the bus. There was a dead silence. No one would look at me. Even Mr. Byers, the driver. I sat down by myself. Usually Ben and I would sit together, as it was the only time during the school day that we'd see each other except in passing. It never bothered him to sit by me, even though he was so much older than me. Most seniors would rather die than be seen paying attention to their kid brothers. I had never thought about it much before. The seat next to mine stayed empty all the way to the school, about forty-five minutes. Everyone was whispering. Somehow having my brother kill himself was kind of a social disgrace.

When Sissy Pavlat got on the bus, she was waving the morning paper. She saw me and took the seat in front of me. She ignored me, but I peeked between the seats and saw what she was reading:

McDougal Mourns Teen Suicide

There was a photograph of Ben. Very stiff and formal. A yearbook photo. And one of me asleep in the Miles parking lot.

"Guess you're a celebrity, J.J.," Sissy said. She didn't turn around to look at me. I knew she'd always had a crush on Ben. She made it sound like it was all my fault.

"Leave me alone," I said.

Suddenly it seemed to hit her, and she started to sob, "I'm sorry, I didn't mean to say that, I didn't, I didn't—" Her cheeks had turned bright red. It made her freckles more pronounced.

Her transformation was appalling, somehow. She had always been snotty to me before. I didn't know how to respond. I didn't say anything at all. I watched the fields of corn unreeling.

Sissy said, "Please speak to me, J.J. I'm scared. I mean, you know, d-death."

"*You're* scared!"

"Oh, I'm sorry, I feel so selfish. I mean, like, you

must really be suffering, and I'm going on about—"

"Quit apologizing," I said. "Don't even talk to me."

There was a camera crew in the hallway. A woman —dark hair, big nose, fake smile—with a microphone kind of bore down on me. "Any reason for the suicide?" she said. She was very nicely dressed, and every strand of her hair was in place, even though it was windy outside. As though it had been glued on. I recognized her vaguely. She had covered the flood over in Kearny County last summer.

"Please leave me alone," I said softly.

She turned to the camera with a look of plastic grief. "For now," she said, "the death of this McDougal High School senior is shrouded in mystery. Teenage suicide has acquired the proportions of a national tragedy—"

I didn't listen. I didn't care about whether it was a national tragedy or not. I heard the newswoman's voice, droning on about statistics, about multiple suicides in an Iowa high school, about scientific theories. I walked right past her toward the water fountain at the foot of the stairs that led to Mrs. Hulan's social studies class. I took off my backpack and stooped to get a drink. When I looked up, a video camera was staring me in the face.

"Benjamin's younger brother, local video game champion Jeremiah Johnson Madigan—"

"No one calls me that and lives," I said. I stared wildly around me. Maybe none of the other kids had overheard. I hoped not. I knew they would all laugh at me if they knew what the J.J. stood for. And now the whole world was going to find out.

"Come on, kid, be nice. This is television," the cameraman said. He seemed annoyed that he had to be up this early, frustrated that I wasn't cooperating.

"He's not your brother—he's mine!" I screamed.
"It's none of your business what I feel." I tried to calm
down. "And my name is J.J."

Kids were piling onto the stairs, crowding us. I saw
Sissy trying to push out to the front. "Awesome!" she
said. "Go for it! Don't let them push you around."

"Jeremiah Johnson?" someone murmured somewhere. Maybe I just imagined it. But it made me
crazy, thinking how the secret I'd concealed all these
years was out now. I just wanted to hide. I was
ashamed because I couldn't seem to show the symptoms of grief everyone expected me to show. And
because they'd found out my name. It would be all
over the school by midmorning, all over the damn
state by the evening news.

The newswoman reached out her arms to me. I
think she was trying to console me, but all I could
think about was how embarrassing the whole thing
was getting. "Get out of my way," I shouted. I slugged
her with my backpack and threw her against the wall.
Slowly she crumpled to the floor. One of the girls
whipped out an autograph book and dived after her.
The cameraman tried to head me off to get a shot of
my grimacing face. I smashed my fist into his stomach. His equipment crashed onto the floor.

I didn't wait around. I just ran for my life. I ran
down the hallway and out the front door and down
the concrete pathway into the street. No one tried to
stop me. I could imagine the principal making a big
fuss over the newswoman and everyone worrying
about liability insurance. No one came after me. The
advantage of being a fourteen-year-old kid is that no
one ever thinks about you except when you annoy
them. Out of sight, out of mind.

I walked around aimlessly for about an hour. Even-

tually I found myself walking into Mr. Miles's store.
The old man peered at me from behind a cluttered
counter. He scratched his bald spot and adjusted his
horn-rimmed spectacles.

"Shouldn't you be . . ." he began. Then he said,
"Never mind. I won't say a word. I understand." He
winked at me. "You're being so brave. Taking it so
well. Right?" And he gave me a candy bar. "That
what they're all telling you? How well you're taking
it?"

"Thanks a whole lot," I said, but didn't think it.

"Running away?" Mr. Miles said.

Actually, it was the first time it had occurred to me.
Behind Mr. Miles there was a thirteen-inch TV set. A
soap opera was on. A woman was saying something
about "the inheritance, think of the inheritance, don't
throw it all away." Mr. Miles fiddled with it and it
became MTV. "My wife's gone into Lamar for the
day," he said. "No reason I should watch the junk she
watches."

The video was "I Gotta Scratch My Ear," by this
totally weird group, the Senseless Vultures. Part of
the video shows a zany, speeded-up neon-lit city-
scape. It's all seen from the air, and the city looks
kind of like a corpse. Then it shows a flock of vultures,
except they have human faces, the faces of the group.
They're ripping the city apart with their talons. No
one has ever figured out all the words or even if they
are actual words.

Mr. Miles laughed. "L.A.," he said, as the camera
zoomed in and out of the maze of city streets.

"I didn't know you watched—" I began. It was so
strange to be standing in the general store watching
MTV with this dude who was probably a couple of
hundred years old.

"It's my secret. Ours now." He winked again. I got the feeling he knew about what had happened at school. Could the news have come on already? I didn't want to ask him. He went on, "Your brother used to come here all the time." I had never known that. Nervously, I started to eat the candy bar.

"I have an aunt in L.A.," I said.

"Yes. Your Aunt Casey," he said. "The Japanese girl. The one your uncle brought back from the Far East."

"You *know* her?" I said.

"She and her husband—your mom's big brother —used to breeze through the commune sometimes."

"My mom never talks about them."

"I guess not. They never became . . . respectable. Last I heard, after your uncle died, she set herself up as a spiritualist or medium or something, in L.A., you know, catering to crazy rich people. Kazeko. That was her real name. But everyone just called her Casey. Seems like I'm the only one who remembers people fifteen, twenty years ago."

"Yeah." I wasn't sure why Mr. Miles was being so talkative all of a sudden. Normally all he ever did was take my money and give me my change. He was just sorry for me, probably.

"Your brother never forgot her, though," he said.

"What do you mean?"

"The morning it happened, he slipped down to the store—"

"Yeah, Mom sent him with the car to buy some flour," I said. What was the old man getting at?

"He really came to use the phone."

"What are you talking about?" I said. I was uneasy. Mr. Miles seemed to know things about Ben I'd never even heard of. I knew, after Ben left to go to the store, he had never set foot in the house again.

"He always used to call her from here. . . ."

"Call who?"

"Why, your Aunt Casey, of course."

"I think I'd better go." I turned to leave. I didn't want to know any more hidden facts about Ben. I'd had it all figured out when I woke up: as long as I couldn't remember anything, then it wasn't real. But now other people were remembering things and messing up the picture.

Quickly I left the store, not saying good-bye or giving any explanation. The wind was up, kicking up the dust in the parking lot. My eyes smarted. I started walking home. Eventually Mr. Miles's pickup pulled up alongside.

"Get in."

I did. But I didn't talk to him.

"Thought I'd give you a ride. Not many customers this time of day anyways. Took a lunch break."

We took off. Mr. Miles always drove faster than anybody I ever met. I looked out the window. The wind was blowing hard. I hated the wind and the sound of the brittle stalks cracking and the wet, rotting-sweet smell.

"You'll be back," Mr. Miles said. "Bring some of that Pacific sunshine with you, okay?"

"I'm not going anywhere," I said. I remembered what he'd said before, too: *Running away?* "There's nowhere to go."

"Yeah." He rummaged in his pocket (never slowing down) and pulled out a piece of paper. "By the way, he left this for you."

I stared at the piece of notebook paper. It was in Ben's handwriting: completely regular, neat and spidery. All it said was:

The password is Nirvana.

"That's it?" I said.
"Yeah."

After he dropped me off, I ran inside. The news team was gone. Mom was away and so was the baby. Maybe she was at the funeral parlor making arrangements. Dad was probably at the bookstore.

Ben had left a message for me! I raced upstairs. The scrap of paper was clammy because I'd clutched it so hard. I went into his room. The computer was still on. There were books everywhere . . . a whole bunch of stuff on the occult. There was a plastic skull on top of the monitor. I picked it up and put it in a drawer with Ben's underwear. I sat down. I am not a computer whiz. Actually I'm pretty much a klutz when it comes to that stuff. Except video games, of course.

I finally managed to load this one disk that I'd seen him fiddling with a few days before. It whirred, and then the screen said:

HI, J.J. I HOPE YOU REALLY ARE J.J. AND NOT SOME COP SNOOPING AROUND OR SOMETHING. WHY DON'T YOU GIVE ME THE PASSWORD?

NIRVANA, I typed.

EXCELLENT, LITTLE DUDE. I TAKE IT YOU'VE BEEN TO SEE OLD MAN MILES. OKAY. HERE'S THE MESSAGE. FOR YOUR EYES ONLY. WILL SELF-DESTRUCT IN THIRTY SECONDS. ARE YOU READY?

Y, I typed

LOOK FOR ME IN THE FORGETTING PLACE.

The screen went blank. I heard a thunk in the disk drive and I knew that the whole message was being automatically wiped.

Was that all he had to say to me? I knew what the Forgetting Place was. It was his private name for

Nirvana. Nirvana is another of those Oriental philosophy words. True to his middle name, Ben knew everything about that stuff. He once explained it to me. "It's where you are completely still inside," he said, "without desire, without motion. Forever." "You believe in that?" I had said to him. He only shrugged, and laughed.

Why had he called Aunt Casey before shooting himself?

"In a moment," I thought, "I'm going to wake up and he'll be here and this whole nightmare will be over. In a moment, in a moment, in just a tiny moment."

That moment never came, and I started thinking seriously about running away to Los Angeles, land of the zooming lights and the Senseless Vultures. Surely Aunt Casey must know something. There was that yawning gap in my memories, and I had to fill it with something, even if it wasn't the truth. Maybe I just didn't *want* to fill it with the truth.

So like maybe I can find Nirvana, the Forgetting Place. That's what I told myself.

But instead, after running away and having all kinds of adventures like you might see on television, and all kinds of adventures like they'd never dare show on television, I would arrive in a totally different place. The place I would find was as sleazy as a garbage pail and as beautiful as tomorrow. It was as scary as a bad dream and as thrilling as a roller-coaster ride. It was huge and shiny and awesome and terribly desolate.

The name of the place was Burbank.

CHAPTER 2

The Night Before the Funeral

I SAT AROUND in the living room, waiting for someone to get home. I wasn't used to the house being empty, because my mom always tried to get home from the mall early enough to feed us a snack when we got home from school, and the baby farm, I mean the day-care center, only stayed open until three o'clock every day. After a while I tossed a pizza into the microwave and flicked on the television. We have our own satellite dish and I sat playing roulette with the remote control, trying to pick up something different. Most of all I was trying not to think of everything that had happened in the past forty-eight hours. I just sat back on the faded denim sofa and watched disjointed bits of movies and music videos.

The local news came on. I saw that newswoman in front of the school. I tried to change the channel, but I couldn't take my eyes off that screen. She was giving that talk about, you know, the national tragedy and the statistics.

I saw myself walking down the hallway toward the camera. "God," I thought, "I look totally bogus." I saw a thin, pinched-faced kid with mussed-up sandy hair and the beginnings of a slouch, wearing a T-shirt with a Senseless Vultures logo on it, and jeans that

14

looked too new, without any character. I was still wearing those clothes. When was it going to happen, that dreadful scene?

But it never did.

There was a close-up of my face. I was shocked. Because there it was: the look of television anguish. My eyes were sunken and I looked like I'd been crying. A voice-over talked about the dead boy's younger brother, numbed by grief. But that wasn't how I'd been feeling at all! I wanted to scream. Somehow they'd taken my true feelings from me and shown me a stranger even to myself. "I hope they show me punching out the cameraman," I thought. "I hope they don't give away my real name." They didn't. I guess there was no way they could have used the footage that came next.

Instead they cut to some doctor in a business suit. He was explaining the "problem of teenage suicide" to a bunch of parents in the auditorium. "Sometimes," he was saying, "kids today just feel that the world is such an appalling place that they can't stand to grow up in it. It's a malaise that's sweeping through our whole society, a kind of defeatism. We have to support these kids, we have to look for the signs."

But that had nothing to do with Ben. Ben didn't think the world was appalling. Ben loved to be alive. Didn't he? I should know, I was closer to him than anyone in the world . . . but now I was starting to think that I didn't know him at all.

I watched the faces of those parents, I saw them fidgety, trying to look serious. Yeah, trying to be full of that TV grief. Did they know I was watching them? They must have had that meeting the night I slept in Mr. Miles's parking lot. I stared at them. I knew what they were thinking: "Poor Madigans. Kid must have been a stranger to them all this time. It could never happen to me, not in a million years."

"This has nothing to do with my brother," I thought. "Malaise, yeah, right. If they blame society, they can get out of blaming themselves."

I changed the channel. They were showing one of those low-budget *Rambo* clones. This dude was running around a paddy field with an M-16 wasting people. Ben always used to say, "Those shows are stupid. They have nothing to do with real violence," and he'd make fun of me for watching them. I started to feel all strange because of how the gore on the TV screen didn't smell the same way as it had done out in the woods. I switched quickly to a music video station and turned it up real loud so I could stop thinking.

Through the window I saw the mailman drive up, so I went out to the box to get it. I came back in and started sorting it out to pass the time. There was business stuff: *Publishers Weekly*, a bunch of catalogs, and something about a booksellers' convention. There was a pile of junk. Also, there was a letter for Ben from some institute in California, the Webb Foundation for Psychic Research. My heart started pounding.

I couldn't help myself. I opened the letter.

"Dear Mr. Madigan," it read. "Your test results are interesting enough to warrant further investigation. Please call"—there was an 800 number— "for an appointment." I was more bewildered than ever.

There was a postcard for him too. It was sort of a collage of palm trees, the Hollywood sign, a few other famous sights. On the other side was scrawled: "Ben: Don't take those tests too seriously. They'll drive you crazy! Casey."

I let the card fall onto the kitchen table. He'd never said anything to me about corresponding with Aunt Casey! But now this confirmed what old man Miles had said. I took the letter from the psychic place and Aunt Casey's card and I stuffed them in the pocket of my jeans.

Don't take *what* too seriously?

I went back into the living room, flipped through all the channels several more times, paused on a soap opera. I didn't really watch it. I just sat there, letting the pizza grow cold, racking my brains to try to figure out what it all meant.

And still there was that hole in my memory . . . was I just too scared to look into it? I wanted to remember and I didn't want to remember at the same time.

Psychic tests . . . my aunt, the Japanese medium . . . mysterious phone calls and notes . . . suicide. It didn't make much sense to me.

I wasn't surprised Ben would be into any of those subjects. He loved anything weird. And if he got interested in something, it would get to be an obsession, and he'd stop at nothing to get the information he wanted.

Last summer he'd been toying with ESP. He had these cards that he'd ordered from some mail-order place. They showed stars, triangles, squares, circles, shapes like that. He showed them to me one day by the river. There was an abandoned shack we used to go to sometimes. The windows had no glass and it was so hot where the sunlight streamed in that the planks scorched our bare feet.

On the opposite bank of the Arkansas River there is a nondenominational cemetery. Nondenominational means that people who don't belong to any religion can pretty much have the ceremony done any way they want. The place is called Starry Havens. Sometimes we would watch people being buried there and try to identify what religion they belonged to, or thought they ought to belong to. Even on a clear day you couldn't see very much because of all the cottonwoods, though the river is narrow enough to swim across.

"They have this Astroturf they use instead of real grass," he said, "and they have this high-tech thing that like cranks the coffin into the ground."

"Weird," I said. They were Catholics this time, I thought.

He whipped out those cards I was talking about then, and said, "Here, try this. Look, I have to pick one and concentrate hard on it, and you have to try to read my mind." He showed them to me one by one. Then he shuffled them and pulled one out.

"Star."

"Wrong. What about this one?"

"Um . . . circle."

"Guess you don't have any weird powers, little dude," he said, laughing. "Here, do it to me."

"Okay." I took them from him.

"Square."

"Yeah."

"Circle."

"Yeah."

"Star."

"Yeah."

"You're . . . no, you're just saying that."

"Wait, there's some trick, isn't there? Cards are marked or something."

"Nuh-uh."

I picked another card.

"Star again."

"Wrong," I said, relieved somehow.

"Fooled you! I knew it was a triangle all the time."

"What! They *are* marked." I threw them back at him. "You're just not the superpower type," I said.

"How do you know?"

"Remember when you tried to raise up a demon after reading that book by James Blish, *Black Easter* or something? You made me kill a toad. Look, we never got all the chalk marks off the floor of this place." The designs Ben had drawn still clung to the old wood. They must have been a year old. "It didn't work, any more than that interstellar communicator you tried to build out of Dad's broken stereo equipment worked."

Ben just laughed, gathered up the cards, and tossed them in the air. I watched them fall, brilliant white in the shaft of summer light that pierced the shadows of our secret hideout. "You hate to believe in magic, don't you?"

"I don't like it, I don't understand it, and if it's just some retarded party trick, you ought to tell me."

"So you can allay your terror of the unknown, little brother?"

"Come on, quit making me nervous."

He looked away, out, across the still river. "Think they're about done burying whoever."

"It's so hazy."

"The whole world shimmers, blurs, dissolves, and you glimpse the edges of other universes." He stared hard into my eyes, like a hypnotist. Maybe it worked, because I didn't move a muscle, I felt rooted to those rotting planks.

"Wish there'd be a wind, just a little breeze. It's like a microwave in here."

"That tacky cemetery," Ben said, real serious suddenly, "is one of the gateways to the Forgetting Place."

There was something frightening about him when he talked like that. "Let's go swimming," I said, and broke free of his eerie gaze.

"Race you."

Replaying that scene in my mind, I kept thinking, "Should I have guessed, even then, that something was wrong?" Then, as the anger welled up in me again, "How did he expect me to know? Damn it, I don't have any superpowers, I can't read minds."

I heard his name suddenly. I opened my eyes, realizing only then that I must have been half asleep. It was that newscast again. It must be the five o'clock news. There I was again, the grief-stricken younger brother.

I moved to turn off the TV.

"No, leave it on." Mom's voice. My parents had come home. My dad was carrying Stephanie in his arms. She was tugging at his beard. They stood there while the whole story ran. They couldn't look away.

My mother looks a lot like Ben, and right now that made me mad. She has his eyes. Her hair's a lot darker than his, though, and right then it was frazzled. She'd used a lot more makeup than usual. The wrinkles around her eyes were gone as if by magic.

"They're TV stars now," I thought bitterly.

The show was even longer than the midday version, because they had a few more experts and they even had Mrs. Hulan reminiscing about when Ben had been a freshman. "He was such an inquisitive boy," she said, "so articulate, so intelligent. I just knew he was going to be someone important when he grew up. Everyone loved him."

Dad said softly, "I heard about what you did in school." I could tell he was trying to be calm.

"They going to suspend me?"

"No. Of course not. But J.J.—" His voice cracked. He moved closer to where I was sitting on the sofa. He put my sister down in the armchair. He smelled sweaty. Maybe he had forgotten to use his deodorant soap. I wasn't sure whether he was about to hug me or not, but somehow I didn't want him to touch me. I flinched, and I saw that I had hurt his feelings, and I didn't know how I could take back that flinch. Rebuffed, Dad stepped back and said, "I wish you'd find a better way of working out your aggression. I mean, I hear you, but—"

"God damn it!" my mother whispered harshly. "If one more piece of sixties psychobabble escapes your lips—"

"Sorry, dear," Dad said. But she'd already scooped up Stephanie and swept up the stairs. Dad said, "Forgive your mother, okay? She's not herself. We'll make it up to you. You'll see."

I slammed my fist against the wall.

"Everyone understands how hurt you're feeling. But you have to give, you have to share." He scratched his beard.

"Your mail is on the kitchen table. I sorted it already." But I didn't tell them about the two pieces addressed to Ben.

Mom came back down to the living room. She was holding a suit on a hanger. "Will this do, do you think?" she said to Dad. "It was always too small for B.B., and it's the right color."

I recognized it suddenly. It was the suit Ben had worn two years ago when he went to receive this award, the high school essay-writing competition. They were going to make me wear it to the funeral.

The funeral was tomorrow, I realized. Tomorrow! Things were moving faster than I could bear. "You can't make me wear that," I said, "it's Ben's."

"But you have to wear black for the funeral—"

"He's not dead! I can't remember anything and it can't be true!" I screamed with terrible desperation. "And I'm not going to wear it because it's his, it's his."

She recoiled. I think she thought I was going to punch her out, too, like the cameraman. Then she sighed. "I can go to Sears and get you a new one, if you like, darling." She sounded tired, so tired.

I didn't answer. I went right by her and up to my room. I slammed the door.

I lay in bed for a few hours. I fell asleep with my clothes on, listening to my parents talking downstairs. Sometimes it seemed like they were fighting, sometimes like they were consoling each other.

When I woke up, there was a brand-new black jacket hanging over my chair, and a pair of black pants, folded, on the seat. My dress shoes had been polished. One of Dad's neckties lay on top of the pants. It was one of the ones with the bookstore logo.

It was barely dawn. No one was up yet.

"No one can see me. No one can hear me," I thought. "Maybe it's time for me to cry."

I tried, but nothing came.

CHAPTER 3

Escape From Starry Havens

BREAKFAST AT THE Madigans' on the morning of the funeral was not what you'd call an uplifting experience. I was sweating in my brand-new suit. I am a bit too tall and too thin, and Mom could never get anything to fit me unless I was there personally.

Mom was in the kitchen cutting up chickens. A bunch of people were supposed to come over after the funeral. I think she hated to have to cope with the family alone. Now I know she was terribly afraid that someone would say it was her fault, because deep down that was what she believed, in a way.

The phone had been ringing all morning. In the middle of breakfast it was for me. I took it in the kitchen, where we were eating.

It was Sissy Pavlat. "Hey, like I'm sorry about giving you such a hard time."

"So what? You could care less."

"That was awesome, when you slugged the cameraman. You think they'll sue? You really showed them. They're such interfering morons."

"I just didn't want to talk about it."

"See you at the funeral."

"Yeah. I guess." She went on jabbering, but I didn't even listen. I held the receiver at arm's length, like a dead rat. Sissy's voice was broadcasting into the kitchen.

My mom grabbed the phone from me and said, "Now, be nice, dear." Then she said to Sissy, "I'm sorry, he's not himself. He's so upset, you know." And glared at me.

"All right," I said very softly. "I'll be nice." I started talking to Sissy. I talked right over her talking because I knew she wasn't really listening to me anyway. "What are you going to wear?" I asked her. "I mean, everyone's going to be there. After all"—I couldn't help myself, I just blurted it out—"it's the social event of the season, isn't it? Like, maybe you can pick out a new boyfriend. Maybe even a senior."

"J.J.!" my mother said, appalled.

" 'Scuse me for living," I said defiantly.

She stared at the phone and the chicken pieces all over the countertop and at me and my kid sister and she started to bawl, grossly, I mean indecently. I backed away.

"What are you crying for?" I said. I couldn't stop myself. "You didn't even know him. You were too busy taking pop psychology classes down in Pueblo."

She shut up. Her silence was even more appalling than her weeping had been. I wanted to apologize, but I knew it was too late. Before I could say anything she had already let it slip out: "If you knew him so well, how come you didn't warn us? How come you didn't stop him?"

We stood there, facing off for an agonizing moment. Sissy's voice was still rattling away on the phone. My mother hung it back up on the wall. It rang again, but neither of us moved to pick it up. After a while, Mom said, "Finish your breakfast, honey."

"Sure."

I sat back down. Dad came in. He had managed to

stuff himself into a sober, impressive-looking dark suit. He looked so serious I almost laughed out loud, until I remembered.

"We're way too early," he said. "It's not for a couple hours yet."

Mom said, "But I have to dress the baby and you know that you have to go ten miles east before you can cross the river."

That was when I realized that Ben was going to be buried in Starry Havens, the tacky cemetery he had once called "the gateway to the Forgetting Place." I wondered if it was part of his plan. I knew there was a plan because of the note from Mr. Miles and the secret password and the message on the computer.

I went back upstairs and tried to straighten out the uncomfortable clothes.

On the way to the funeral, I was sitting in the back of the car with Stephanie. Barren fields stretched endlessly to our right, and to the left was the river. I rocked the baby back and forth, and she fell into a grunting, wheezing sort of sleep.

I tried teasing at the gap in my memory. But I knew I would find nothing.

Mom was saying, "I hope the chicken will be all right. I hope the timer will reset automatically like it should. Only B.B. knows how to handle these high-tech devices properly. Knew."

"For God's sake, Alice, stop talking about the chicken."

"It was on sale. You know, the bulk rate."

My dad veered sharply to avoid an eighteen-wheeler. He'd been drifting toward the middle of the road. I felt this clammy dread climbing up the back of my throat. I just knew he was going to have an accident.

My mom said, "Please drive properly. The baby—"

"How do you expect me to drive? Like a little old Republican lady? Give me some space, Alice!" He looked at her imploringly and she kind of backed off a little.

"Of course. I'm so terribly sorry," my mother said. She was on the verge of crying again, but maybe she was trying not to upset me and Stephanie.

"I hope the chicken's going to be all right," she said softly.

I knew they were getting ready for a fight. I kind of shrank into the back seat, waiting for the storm to come.

"The chicken!" my father screamed. "If only you'd buy that Perdue chicken instead of cut-rate bulk-sale junk, it'd stay tender instead of drying up!"

Stephanie woke up and started crying. "You've woken up the baby," Mom said. "And you don't know how hard it is, budgeting for a family of five, of four, with the kind of money the store brings in. Perdue chicken!"

"You could cut the damn psychology courses."

"I want to do something with my life and not stay here in this backwater surrounded by illiterates."

"You want to do something! You're forty years old! How about figuring out how to keep a chicken from drying out?"

I couldn't stand it anymore. I put the baby down. "Let me out of the car!" I screamed.

We screeched to a halt. Not on the shoulder. Right in the middle of the road. "You need to go, baby?" my mother said. "You should have gone before we left."

"No, Mother, I am not suffering from a bladder control problem," I said, noticing suddenly that I was starting to sound kind of like Ben. "But you're grown-ups. You're driving to a funeral and fighting about chicken. Don't you understand anything? Ben's dead, you guys, he's totally dead. I tried to like not believe it, but it didn't work." I opened the door. "I'm not going to the funeral. You're grown-ups, you know. You're not supposed to go to pieces, you're supposed to be strong so us kids can go to pieces." I got out and started walking away.

I heard my dad say, "Let him go. He has to work this out himself, somehow. We're not helping." I looked back. I saw him. He seemed totally dominated by those squeaky-clean, shiny black clothes of his. He looked defeated. They pulled away and I could see that they had started to fight again.

I walked home with the dust blowing into the fresh sharp creases of my new suit. But although my parents never found out, I did go to my brother's funeral, in a way.

It was a couple of miles along Route 50 to the house. When I got there, I heard my brother's voice calling me from upstairs: "Are you there, J.J.? Are you there, J.J.?"

I froze. The voice kept repeating itself over and over. I rubbed my eyes and shook the dust from my clothes and threw the jacket over the sofa. Then I ran upstairs.

It was only the computer. The voice-synthesizing program. I don't know how Ben had done it. It was driving me crazy. I jabbed the return key, hoping to turn the voice off.

The screen went into a frenzy of colors, then said:
HI, LITTLE BROTHER. I KNEW YOU'D NEVER MAKE IT TO THE FUNERAL. WAIT A MINUTE. AM I SURE IT'S YOU?

My hair started to stand on end. It felt cold in the room, deathly cold. My hands were shaking as they typed the word NIRVANA.

OF COURSE I'M ONLY GUESSING, the computer continued, BUT I'VE ALWAYS BEEN A GOOD GUESSER. YOU MIGHT SAY I'M PSYCHIC. I CAN SEE THE FUTURE SOMETIMES. I SAW YOU RUNNING DOWN THE ROAD, AWAY FROM STARRY HAVENS. MAYBE I DREAMED IT. BUT JUST IN CASE YOU'RE REALLY THERE, HERE'S THE NEXT PART OF THE MESSAGE.

BENJAMIN BHAKTI MADIGAN, HIS LAST WILL AND TESTAMENT.

BEING OF A SOUND MIND, I HEREBY BEQUEATH ALL MY TREASURES TO MY LITTLE BROTHER, JEREMIAH JOHNSON.

THE FULL MOON WILL STRIKE THE PLANK.

I LOVE YOU, LITTLE DUDE.

THE WORLD GROWS DIM. I SEE NO MORE. FAREWELL.

I heard the familiar whir of erasure. I tried to get the message back up. I tried to catalog the disk. Nothing worked. Downstairs, the phone was ringing. I ignored it.

I stripped and put on some decent clothes: another Senseless Vultures T-shirt and my favorite jeans that I had worn down until they felt soft and comfortable. My jeans still had the two pieces of mail in them, the card from Aunt Casey and the letter from that institute.

Then I went out to the shack by the river.

And watched them bury my brother.

They were so far away, they were more like action figures than people. The whole of McDougal must have been there. The cemetery was swarming. I thought I could make out the principal of the school.

A line of cars was pulling in, wiggling like segments of a metal millipede. I recognized the van from the local TV station too. I watched a while longer. "This is as close as I ever want to get to Ben's death," I told myself. I meant it too. "You got no right to do this to me! You'd have been able to handle our parents when they got like that. Fighting over the damn chickens." What did he mean by leaving those messages in the computer? Did he really foresee the whole thing? I stretched out on the boards with my head against the wall and tried to figure out what the hell my big brother had meant.

What treasures?

What full moon striking the plank?

What was I going to do?

I heard cars pulling in. "I'm not going back. I'm not facing them," I thought. "They'll just have another scene. In front of all those people."

I heard voices now. They were hushed, conciliatory. "I'm so sorry, Mrs. Madigan. So terribly sorry." They must be in the backyard, right by the wood that obscured the view of the river. I thought I could smell fried chicken wafting through the odor of rotting leaves. I was hungry as a horse but I was too scared to go back inside.

Now there were footsteps. I bolted the door. I couldn't see who it was, and they couldn't see me. The only window was out over the river.

"I'm not coming out," I said.

"We're worried about you, son," my father said. "People are asking. Please. What do you want me to say? I'll say anything."

I unbolted the door and opened it just a crack. "Daddy—" I said, like a little boy.

"I can't stand it," he said. He hugged me hard, like

a kid with a teddy bear. "Will you come inside soon?"

I said, quoting his own words back at him, "I just need to, like, work it out." I tried to smile.

"I brought you a candy bar," he said, pulling one out of his pocket. I took it. It was warm and mushy. "We don't mean those things, son. We hear you, we love you."

"Yeah," I said, unyielding. Then I said, "I just need a few more hours. I'll be here. Don't worry about me. I just need to be alone. I'll come back real soon."

I didn't.

One time, when the sun was setting, I crept back to the house and hid in the bushes bordering the back-yard. The yard was full of people. They were all dressed in black. There was a table with food on it. Sissy Pavlat was talking to my mother as she cut her a slice of cake.

"There was something so special about him," she was saying. "Maybe this thing can like bring us all together somehow."

My mother went on cutting.

"Where's J.J.?" Sissy said. "I feel so awful. I think I hurt him."

I turned back. I think they heard the rustle of my leaving, because I could hear Sissy pause for a moment before plunging headlong into conversation again.

I waited for the sun to go down. I had an idea of what Ben meant about the plank in the moonlight. The shack became dark, but there was a flashlight hanging on the wall, and I used it.

The noises from the house grew quiet.

Maybe I dozed off. One minute it was getting dark, the next it was pitch-black. I shook the flashlight. I must have worn out the batteries. I looked at the window. It was cloudy. I couldn't see the moon. What was the use of psychic powers if you couldn't get the weather right? I was tired, so tired. I was about ready to go back inside when the clouds broke, and a beam of moonlight shot into the darkness and illuminated a single floorboard. I gulped.

Tentatively I nudged it. It gave and I eased it out.

There was a Jiffy Bag beneath it. It was one of the ones publishers use to send single-order books. The mailing label was addressed to the store, from the Sterling Book Company in New York. I could just about read it in the moonlight. The bag was lumpy. I wanted to empty it out, but first I had to replace the board, because that was the only place I could lay it out on and still see.

First there was something I had always coveted: my brother's CD Walkman. I felt a surge of pleasure at holding it in my hands, but guilt welled up. I almost dropped it. There were a couple of laser disks, includ-' ing one of the Senseless Vultures' latest album, *Planet Smashers*. I held it up to the light. Tygh Simpson, the group's lead singer, looked back at me, his face made up like an Oriental mask.

I opened it up and inside, next to the rainbow-shiny disk, were two fifty-dollar bills.

I shook the bag to see what else was in it.

First—well, you know that kid's game where they have these playing cards, a bottom half and a top half, and you get to match the pig's head with the duck's feet? A lot of laughs when you're about five years old? There were two cards, top and bottom. But they weren't ducks and pigs. Each was a tarot card. They use them for telling fortunes. I don't know much about them, but Ben, of course, had a deck of them in his collection of occult objects. They were the top and bottom of two different cards, but they had been sliced precisely, with an X-acto knife probably. They fit together seamlessly. I recognized them. One is called the Hanged Man and it shows this dude hanging upside down by one foot. That was the bottom half, so you saw his head and torso up to his waist. The other card was Death. A hooded skeleton brandishing a scythe.

There was also a scrap of paper. It seemed to have been torn out of a letter. It was in Aunt Casey's handwriting. There were bits and pieces of words, but only one complete word in the middle of the paper: "Sumidagawa."

That was all.

I turned the paper upside down, I tried peering through it, but I couldn't get anything else out of it. The word looked like it might be Japanese, but I couldn't tell. I looked at everything I had: the CD player, the disks, the piece of paper, the hundred dollars, the mail. What was my brother trying to tell me?

One thing was for sure. I couldn't get any answers here. My parents would come back with some pop psychology cliché. Doctors on television would tell me all about the teenage suicide phenomenon. My friends at school wouldn't know what to say to me and they'd back off as if I were a leper, or say something harmless and nice while trying to make their getaway.

Ben left messages for me, not for any other person. That meant that there was only one person who could solve the riddle. Me. And sitting in that dark shack by the river in the moonlight, arranging and rearranging the miscellaneous objects on the plank, I finally understood what the next step had to be.

It must be what my brother wanted. And because I loved Ben more than anyone, and because I still yearned to be just like him, I knew I would do it. I didn't think about the price.

I put everything I had into the Jiffy Bag.

I trudged a ways along the river so as to avoid my house, and then cut through the woods to reach the main road.

Then I started to walk to California.

CHAPTER 4

"I don't think we're in Kansas anymore"

THE MOON WAS back behind trees and clouds. The road was dusty, dark, and unearthly quiet. I had the CD player slung on my jeans and I listened to the Senseless Vultures. I didn't bring my watch, but I could tell how much time was passing by counting the number of times the first cut on the album came up. There wasn't one car on the road for the first two hours.

It was good to walk with the music pounding in your ears. You didn't have to think, and the beat kept your feet moving, step after step after step. I took the first five miles or so—up to the *Welcome to Colorado* sign—without feeling a thing, but I was getting hungry. The next five were torture. It was chilly, and all I had on was the T-shirt. "How many more miles to California?" I thought. "A couple thousand . . . I could get there in a couple months. . . ."

Suddenly, out of nowhere, this pickup truck screeched to a stop beside me. A shadowy figure beckoned to me. I was scared at first. People who pick up hitchhikers . . . well, I'd heard stories. I thought of just running on, but I was so tired I knew I was going to drop. Quickly I thought up a plan.

I put the headphones around my neck and climbed into the pickup. It was totally dark inside. Even the

34

instrument panel was dim, and this dude was
wrapped from head to foot. He even had a scarf over
his face. It was too late to get out. He'd already
started the truck.

I jabbed two fingers into his ribs. "If you're thinking of molesting me," I said, "forget it. I got a gun."

"Oh, God . . . take my wallet . . . I've only got a
couple bucks in it anyway . . . oh, you seemed like
such a nice kid. . . ."

I hesitated. Maybe he was on the level, maybe not. I
jabbed harder. "I know what you're like, you dudes
who pick up kids in the middle of the night," I said.
"Just keep driving."

"All the way to California?"

"How did you know—"

I noticed the scarf winding itself loose from the
man's face. Suddenly I recognized the horn-rimmed
glasses. "Wait, I know you," I said.

"Damn," Mr. Miles said, "I hoped I'd be able to do
this errand of mercy anonymously."

"You can't take me home! I won't go!"

"Have a candy bar."

"Thanks." My stomach growled. At that moment,
that candy bar was probably the most important
thing in the universe to me. I wolfed it down and was
about to toss the wrapper out of the window.

"Don't litter." He wagged his finger at me.

"What the hell are you doing out here at this time
of night?" I said.

"Mild-mannered Horatio Miles, McDougal shop-
keeper, ain't quite what he seems," he said, nodding.
"Maybe I was out watching for Halley's comet. Maybe
I was driving back from a witches' sabbath after
sacrificing innocent babes on the altar of the Evil
One. Maybe I was communicating with aliens. Or
with the dead."

He gunned the accelerator. We must have been doing eighty-five, ninety. "Don't go so fast!" I yelled, exhilarated in spite of myself, with the wind roaring in my ears.

"Why not?" he shouted back. "You afraid I'm so ancient and frail I'm going to have a heart attack? How old d'you think I really am, a hundred? Hey, but you need some excitement. The days of leaving Kansas by tornado are over. This Chevy's a lousy replacement, but high tech's always been a poor replacement for magic!"

"You're crazy!"

He only crackled like a wicked witch. "Considering the evidence in toto, I don't think we're in Kansas anymore!"

I rolled my eyes.

A few minutes later, he cursed. "Missed Lamar by a good ten miles!" The pickup stopped dead. "Happens all the time with these dinky towns." Then he started backing up.

"You're gonna back up ten miles?"

We did. I had to close my eyes, it was so stomach-turning. But Mr. Miles only laughed the whole time.

It was dawn as we pulled into Main Street. The Madonna of the Trail, which is a statue of a pioneer woman with a shotgun and a baby on her hip, seemed to glower ferociously in the ruddy light. "Let's stop at the Daylight Donut," Mr. Miles said.

Mr. Miles drank four or five cups of coffee and I munched slowly on a chocolate-covered doughnut.

I had barely finished my doughnut when Mr. Miles looked at his watch. "Uh-oh," he said. "You only have five more minutes."

I panicked. "You taking me home now?"

"No, you silly boy. That's when your bus leaves."

He pulled something out of his pocket. "Here's your ticket. No, don't bother to thank me, I was just keeping it for you."

"Ben?" I said wonderingly.

He chuckled. "B.B. is a very special person," he said.

"He *is*?" I said. What was Mr. Miles trying to tell me? Maybe it was some kind of hint. I stared at him but I couldn't understand his expression. I guess I was reading too much into it.

"I am truly sorry it ended this way." He took off his glasses and wiped a tear from his eye. "He means a lot to me," he said. That was more than Mom and Dad had said about Ben in the past couple days.

"Thank you," I said, "for not weirding out on me like my parents did." He seemed to be the only person who understood why I couldn't break out in fits of weeping.

He said, "Keep the watch." He took it off and put it on my wrist. It was one of those things with a compass and a barometer and God knows what else. When I tried to thank him, he put a finger on my lips and said, "Save your breath, kid."

He walked me to the Trailways station, which was a grimy-looking, dinky place with peeling paint and a dirty floor. The bus pulled in. I got on and went to the back. When I looked out of the window, Mr. Miles had already vanished.

"I'm dreaming," I thought. I didn't even know Aunt Casey's address.

The next few days were all the same. The scenery changed, and my clothes became dirtier and smellier, and different people got on and off, and sometimes I had to hang around for a few hours in a sleazy waiting room, monopolizing some video game.

Going to the bathroom was about the scariest thing about the trip. I never knew what I was going to see. The first time I went was somewhere in New Mexico and this drunk dude was trying to sell me something. I almost called my parents.

It was around three in the morning. I picked up the phone and I dialed the number, but the operator came on and asked me for $4.90 in exact change, so I lost my nerve. I tried the bathroom again but the dude was still in there, sitting on the sink and leering at me in the dingy light.

After that I held it for like ten hours. But in the end I had to go. In Arizona, I think.

I hardly noticed the mountains or the desert or the junk food. It seemed like from the moment I stepped on the bus in Lamar, I had stepped away from the real world and into a territory of shadows and blurred images. I could close my eyes and hear Ben's voice again: "The whole world shimmers, blurs, dissolves, and you glimpse the edges of other universes." I was beginning to see it happen. I remembered his eyes, serious and stone-cold.

I always put the Jiffy Bag on the aisle seat so no one would want to sit there. It was never more than a few inches from my hand. Sometimes I would clutch it firmly in my lap. I didn't trust anyone. With my eyes closed I could imagine Ben was sitting next to me on the bus. And I'd talk to him—not aloud, because I didn't want anyone to think I was talking to myself. I didn't feel like being hauled off to a loony bin.

"You're not really dead, are you?" I'd say. "You're still talking to me. Through the clues, through the computer messages, through Mr. Miles."

He didn't answer me. Sometimes I could swear I felt him there, though. When you're really close to someone, you get used to the way they smell, even the way they part the air around them. And I'd say, "See? You're not dead. And somehow, someday, I'm going to understand those messages and I'm going to be able to reach you . . . wherever you are . . . even if it's the Forgetting Place."

And I'd remember bits and pieces of conversations: "I wonder if Mom and Dad know about your namesake, Liver-eatin' Johnson, the famous Indian killer. I found it in this data base that I accessed." Or: "I really like her, but I don't want her to find out that I'm into telepathy." Or, this with a wry smile: "Are we going to be around when they nuke the world?"

In Arizona I was almost certain that I heard his voice. But when I opened my eyes, it was a fat Indian with long hair who never smiled in all the hours I watched his face. I saw sand and cactuses and more sand, and I sipped a cactus soda that a woman handed me to try. I didn't like it.

Then it seemed that I fell into a long sleep, only I wasn't quite asleep, I was just lulled into a trance by the constant motion of the bus. I remembered when Ben and I rode our bikes to Mr. Miles's store. It must have been years ago because Ben's voice hadn't even changed yet.

Mr. Miles was hunched down, looking for something behind one of the shelves, and Ben just blurted out, "It's behind the counter, on top of the television set."

Mr. Miles looked at us quizzically. "How'd you know I was looking for my wallet?" he said.

Ben shrugged. "Just sort of came out, I guess. What do you know." There was an uncomfortable silence, and then Ben said, "She won't last past next week."

That was when Mr. Miles's mother died.

But I couldn't have known that. I just thought it was one of Ben's jokes. But Mr. Miles went all funny-looking, like a bursting balloon. "Why, thank you, Benjamin Bhakti," he said slowly, and that bothered me, because I didn't think Mr. Miles knew what B.B. stood for, and I wondered if he knew my real name. "It's good to know so I can get ready."

I stared from one to the other. They wouldn't meet each other's gaze. Mr. Miles gave us each a candy bar and told us to say nothing. We watched his mother's funeral from the shack.

As I thought of this, I came to realize there must have been some secret they shared, even then. Who was Mr. Miles, really? An alien? Were they studying us or something? It sounded like one of the stories Ben wrote and then concealed in his closet or in a shoe box under his bed.

Or was Mr. Miles some kind of magician? A witch? A sorcerer? "Maybe I was communicating with aliens. Or the dead." That's what he said to me. "He likes to be mysterious," I thought. "He's old and eccentric, but there's nothing supernatural about him. Is there?" It wasn't something I wanted to think about.

Then I woke up in downtown Los Angeles.

I was on Hollywood Boulevard walking aimlessly, with nothing but the clothes on my back and the Jiffy Bag under my arm. I think I was going west. I passed a street named Argyll and a street named Cherokee. It was night and the streets were still full of people —more people than I'd ever seen in my life. And everything was too bright and too jarring, more like a computer simulation than real life. A lot of stores were open. There were a lot of cars. And the way it smelled was something I could never have guessed: it was kind of like gasoline and nachos and flowers all at the same time. I wanted to stop someone and ask for help, but I didn't know what to ask for. I had no idea how I was going to find Aunt Casey at all. The lights, the people, the cars all shimmered as if they weren't quite real.

I stopped at a fast-food place to get a bite. I didn't understand anything on the menu. I might as well have been on Mars. Finally I settled for a teriyaki burrito, which cost $1.29. It didn't taste bad. Kind of like all-mushed-up microwave leftovers.

As I tossed the wrapper in the garbage can, I thought I heard Ben's voice, whispering over the cacophony of the city: "The edges of other universes." I looked up. He was there, I was sure of it, standing next to this gigantic dude who was dressed as a ninja, in front of the glass front of a bookstore. . . .

"Ben—" I cried out.

I blinked. He wasn't there anymore. But I felt close to him. I walked faster, toward the ninja, who was like an advertisement for the bookstore, I guess: Far East Book Niche. All I could see were his eyes behind all that black cloth.

"Sir—" I said to him.

"Wanna buy a book?"

"Uh, sure."

He bowed to me and opened the door of the bookstore. I was too intimidated to walk away, so I went inside and pretended like I was looking at the bookshelves. There was a bunch of stuff in Japanese and Chinese (I think) and language books and books about flower arranging and Buddhism. Ben would have loved the place. It had a weird, sweet smell. I saw that it came from a brazier of burning incense.

There was like this sunken part in the middle with great big pillows and three or four Siamese cats. People were sitting there reading books. They were utterly quiet. One of them was a guru-type dude wearing a funny robe with a dot in the middle of his forehead. He was reading a *Star Trek* novel. The cats kept flopping on top of him, but he would kind of wiggle his lap and the cat would bounce onto the floor, which was covered with this powerful-smelling dried straw kind of stuff. There was also a sort of suburban-housewife-looking person who was reading *Esoteric Oriental Secrets of Love and Magic.*

The incense started seeping into me and messing with my mind. I didn't feel right. This sure wasn't anything like Kansas.

I was probably a lot more scared than I wanted to admit to myself. Nothing moved at all in the store. Now and then the guru dude wheezed as he turned the page, and once I heard him whisper, "Warp factor five!" The place was chilly, too, with an air conditioner going full blast, even though it wasn't that hot outside. Anxiously I looked around. Then I turned to one of the shelves and scrutinized the spines of the books.

Someone poked me in the small of my back.

I jumped. The Jiffy Bag slid out of my hands. I scrunched down to pick it up, and my head bumped against someone's head. "Sorry," I said, trying to retrieve the scattered stuff.

It was the guru. "Sorry to scare you," he said. "I will soon be closing, you know. After midnight, only by appointment."

He was on his hands and knees helping me find everything. He picked up the piece of paper with the word *Sumidagawa* on it.

"Oh, is that what you are looking for?" he said. "In

the Japanese literature section. Maybe you are wanting translation?"

"I don't even know what it is," I said.

"I will be coming right back. If you please, relax on one of the cushions."

I did, putting the headphones back on. I had heard the album so often I felt that I was on the verge of understanding the words of the songs. But not quite.

Ooaaaoo aaa uuu I'm a tell you uaaoeeii

The man came back with a book under his arm. He shouted, "Is this it?"

"I can hear you fine," I shouted back, and then I suddenly remembered to turn down the CD player.

I looked at the book. *"Five Japanese Noh Plays. Translated by Lex Nakashima.* What's a Noh play?"

"Ancient Japanese literature. That'll be $29.95."

"Holy—"

"Culture is costing money these days, young man."

"Let me look at it first."

"Okey-doke."

I read the flap copy. It said something about how these plays are hundreds of years old and used to be performed in the courts of Japan, and everyone wears masks. I flipped through and saw pictures of the masks.

Then I saw a paragraph about Sumidagawa: "A woman, driven mad by the death of her child, waits for the ferryman to take her across the Sumidagawa River to her child's grave. Finally she communes with the spirit of the child. . . ."

My heartbeat quickened. I must be on to something. A river, a ferryman, a grave on the other side . . . communicating with the dead. This was my life too: the Arkansas River, Starry Havens across the water, messages from Ben. Was this the message my brother meant for me?

I said, "$29.95 . . ." I was thinking of how many times I could go to Burger King for that amount of money.

"It is yours."

"Huh? Why?"

"You are having in your eyes the light of one who seeks," the guru said.

"You sound like my dad when he's in one of his sixties moods."

The guru laughed. "I suppose this way of talking is out of fashion, isn't it? Well, what shall I be saying instead? Awesome! It's casual. Totally gnarly."

"A Valley guru?" I said, laughing.

"Keep the book anyway. Let us say it is my concession to *bhakti* for the day."

You could have knocked me over with a floppy disk. "Bhakti?" I said.

"The proper application of *jñana*, or knowledge, is to integrate it into the mind and let it issue out in action. It then becomes *bhakti*, or devotion."

I nodded, trying to look as though I understood everything he said.

"Actually, it's just one of those Oriental philosophy buzzwords," the guru said. "I'm not believing in any of that stuff myself, but the customers, they are expecting a little show for their money, isn't it? These days, I myself am only reading science fiction. Enjoy the book. I must be closing up, as I said before. Be off with you!"

Suddenly I didn't want to leave. I'd been nervous when I first came in, but I was even more uneasy about going back out there. I had to think of something to ask, to stall for time. I said, "What time is it?"

"Ha, ha! Must be a deep philosophical question, since I see very well you are wearing a wristwatch."

"Oh, yeah, I forgot. Oh . . . oh . . . how would I go about looking for someone? Someone in a strange city, I mean?" Suddenly I felt so frail. I had an urge to ask him to call my parents for me, but I steeled myself. The answer to my quest seemed so tantalizingly near. . . .

"Who do you need?" the guru said.

"My aunt," I said. He looked at me oddly, so I lied. "She was supposed to pick me up at the Trailways station but I got here a day early by mistake." He raised an eyebrow. I racked my brains for a better story, and then remembered something I'd overheard Ben say once, and said, "It's the date line. I crossed the date line, you see."

"Ah, you must have come from India," the guru said. "Perhaps when you go back you will be looking up an aunt of mine?"

Too late I remembered that the date line is in the middle of the Pacific Ocean. I just tried to shrug it off.

"It's okay, kid. There's a phone outside. Call directory assistance. Here's a quarter."

"Oh, thank you, sir," I said, frantically gathering up my belongings and trying to stuff the book into the Jiffy Bag.

"Don't spend it on video games!" he said, as he ushered me to the door. "And, my child, I think you had better take a bath." In a strange kind of way, the guru reminded me of Mr. Miles. I saw him wrinkling his nose as he locked up the front door, and somehow it made me laugh. I had a feeling I'd be coming back to that bookstore.

CHAPTER 5

Zombies in Limousines

DIRECTORY ASSISTANCE HAD never heard of Kazeko Herrity. I hung up and tried again, spelling it very carefully. Didn't work. I slammed the phone down hard.

"C'mon, I don't have all night."

I whipped around to see who it was. I saw this kid—maybe my age—silhouetted against flashing neon lights that advertised a kung fu movie. The kid had a Mohawk a good six inches high. It was purple or blue. I couldn't tell in the artificial light. It must have been stiffened with Krazy Glue. He had very sharp features and was wearing a leather jacket, even though it had to be stifling hot. He had a human skull painted on his left cheek, and, going through it, a bolt of lightning. "Wow," I said, "you must be a Vultures fan. You look totally radical."

"*Radical?*" the kid said, sneering. "Who says *radical* anymore? You from Kansas or something?"

"Yes," I said, feeling defiant. "Wanna make something of it?"

"Knives? Guns? Knuckles?"

"I don't care," I said. "I'm about to give up anyway."

46

I thought he was going to kill me. Instead, the kid said, "Shame on you, beating up on a girl."

I stared stupidly for a moment, then said, "Like, uh, I'm sorry, you know." I was so embarrassed I wanted to crawl back into the phone booth.

"Yeah. Can't tell the men from the women these days."

"That's what they used to say about my parents."

"Ex-hippies?"

"Yeah."

"My sympathies."

"I'm J.J. Madigan," I said, offering to shake her hand.

She looked at it for a second, then kind of touched it in a perfunctory way. "I'm Zombie. Zombie McPherson." She spat out a huge wad of rainbow-colored gum and tossed it into a trash can.

"That can't be your real name."

"So? What kind of a name is J.J.?"

"All right. *Touché.*"

"Well, like who are you trying to call?"

"My aunt."

"Ran away from Kansas?"

"What's this with Kansas? There's nothing wrong with Kansas. That's got nothing to do with anything."

"My sympathies. I went to Kansas once."

"What are you doing here? I mean, it's so late and all."

"What do you think?" Zombie said. "I'm on the street same as you. It could be worse. I could be pushing cocaine. As it is, I only have to lay back and like close my eyes."

Suddenly I understood what she was saying. I was shocked, genuinely shocked. On the other hand, I'd never met a real live hooker before. I said, "How can you do something like that? I mean, let people take advantage of you—"

"Why shouldn't they? My own father did," she said matter-of-factly.

"No. Things like that don't happen." I couldn't have heard her right.

She laughed. "For sure, I guess not. I'm happy here, I'm free, I'm me, I don't need anyone."

I didn't think she looked happy at all, or free. What was in her voice was more like anger than happiness. Her blast of emotion was like so intense that it made me nervous. I edged away from her. I wanted to do something for her but she made me terribly afraid. I said, "Well, I guess I have to try calling her again," and turned back to the phone even though I knew it would be useless.

"So what are *you* doing here?" she persisted. "Your father beat up on you? Your mother an alcoholic?"

"No, no, it's nothing like that," I said. "I just came to see my aunt. I'm just, like, visiting."

"From Kansas. With school not out yet. And you don't even know her phone number. Don't give me any of that bull, kid. I've heard it all. Grody parents, drugs, too many suds, you name it. You gotta be running away from something."

I couldn't stand it anymore. "All right, my brother killed himself. I don't know why. There's a lot I don't even remember. Maybe it's my fault. My family's going to pieces. Now leave me alone. Please, just leave me." I was on the verge of tears. But no tears came.

Her expression softened a little. I dialed directory assistance again. "Have you tried the Valley?" she said.

"The Valley? What Valley?"

"You know, as in Valley Girl? Area code 818—"

"Oh, it's not the same area code?" I said, feeling totally retarded.

"You really are from Kansas. Of course it's not the same. Maybe you've noticed that there are a couple more people around here than back home? What a hoynt."

It had never occurred to me that there could be more than one area code in the same city. That was how naïve I was, I guess. Yes, I knew that I was in one of the largest metropolises in the world. But I had only seen about five city blocks so far and I was already on heavy overload.

"What are you gaping at, kid?" Zombie said, grabbing the phone from me. "Here, I'll do it for you. I don't have all night. I got a call to make too. Now, what's this woman's name?"

I told her.

She talked into the phone for a few seconds. "I got the number," she said. "And the address. It's on Magnolia and Damaris. In Burbank. I told you so. No more change? Here, use this," she went on, and plucked a credit card out of her sleeve. "It's my AT&T number. Actually, it's my father's. I stole it."

I took it. "Why are you being so generous all of a sudden?"

"I don't know. Because of your brother, I guess."

I thought of Ben. His face kind of swam up to the top of my mind. Nobody ever thought we looked alike. Strangers could never guess that we were brothers, even. But I always knew I looked like him. If I would rough my hair up some, and purse my lips goofily, and stare off into the distance . . . I'd be just like him.

I felt a twinge of guilt, because I hadn't thought about him for five or ten minutes. I dialed.

It was an answering machine. A woman's voice,

with a trace of a Japanese accent. "Madame Kazeko is unavailable at the moment. Séance hours are by appointment only."

"It's a damn machine," I said, about to hang up in frustration.

The machine said, "Because of unprecedented demand for our services, we can no longer do house calls. By the way, if this is J.J., I'm expecting you."

"She's expecting me," I said. "Is there a bus or subway or something I can catch?"

"Bus! Subway! You really are from Kansas, or at the very least another planet."

"I'll take a cab."

"It'll probably cost you thirty bucks to go to Burbank from here. Don't be ridiculous. But . . . I have an idea." She took the phone from me and dialed another number and talked for a little while. Then she hung up and said, "About ten minutes. Then —Burbank or bust."

"Why are you doing this for me?"

"How should I know?" she said with the same anger that had made me back away from her before. I was sorry I'd asked.

We sat on a bench under a palm tree waiting. Ten minutes went by, and then ten more. "Gum?" Zombie said.

"Thanks."

"Tell me about your brother."

"Don't want to."

"Why did he—"

"I really don't know," I said. I wished she would not try to probe into my private darkness.

"Maybe he was like getting his jollies, you know? Lots of guys like to strangle themselves for kicks.

Then, one day, they don't disentangle themselves in time. I saw on TV that some expert was saying that a lot of teenage guys waste themselves that way."

"That's gross! Ben wasn't like that at all!" But it occurred to me that I had thought I knew my brother better than anyone in the world, and now I was finding out so much more about him, piece by piece.

"Besides, he didn't hang himself, he shot himself," I said. "And it's none of your damn business."

"Blows that theory," she said.

I turned away and watched the cars go by. I chewed gum while she talked, mostly to herself.

"I have a good time, mostly," she said. "It's a living. And I'm tough."

"You sound like you're trying pretty hard to convince me you're okay," I said at last.

"I envy him," she said. "I really do. You try to see what's going to happen, sometimes you seem to see it like so clearly, and you see there's no place to go anymore. At least he had the guts to get out on his own steam."

I said nothing.

"Did you cry a lot, when he like croaked?"

"No! I didn't cry at all!" I said, so she'd get out of that dark place inside me. "I was totally heartless, stone-cold. I walked out on all of them."

"You're just like me," she said, nodding like a wise guru. "Don't let it touch you. We're strong, you and me. We can take it."

That made me mad. I wasn't anything like her. "I don't like you," I said.

She shrugged. "Nobody else does."

It was two in the morning when this awesome limousine pulled up to the curb. It seemed to fill the whole block. It was creamy-white, and it had some

kind of metallic Godzilla monster as a hood ornament. And I was sure I'd seen it before somewhere. In
a dream maybe.

Then this totally tall black dude in a white suit and
dark glasses stepped out. "Your taxi awaits," he said.
When I saw him, I just knew what he had to be. I
mean, I'd watched enough television to know what
dudes in white suits and dark glasses in limousines
who hang out with teenage girls *do* for a living. I just
stood there with my mouth wide open, not daring to
get into the car.

"Well, get in," Zombie said. "Like, it's a free ride."

"I'm not getting into the same car as a —" I pointed
from Zombie to the man, back and forth. Zombie and
the black dude looked at each other, puzzled. Then
Zombie suddenly started laughing.

"You've been watching too much television, dude,"
Zombie said. "This isn't a pimp. I don't have one of
those cockroaches. I operate independently. This is
Justin Casper, my friend, who happens to work as a
chauffeur. I have connections. Justin happens to be
the man I love."

I had felt really stupid many times already that
night, but this really took the cake. When I got a good
look at him, I realized he was younger than I'd
originally thought, probably only nineteen or twenty.
Meekly I got into the back seat. Zombie got in with
me. There was a television, a refrigerator, and a
telephone in the shape of a little electric guitar
hanging from one side.

The television was playing a music video with the
Vultures on it, but it was one I'd never seen before.
Fascinated, I turned the volume up. Zombie had this
glassy-eyed look on her face as she watched Justin put
the car into drive.

"Where to, baby?" Justin said.

"Magnolia and Damaris," Zombie said.

"We'll have to race. You're lucky I could make it at all. But they're having a heavy-duty overtime session at the studio. Tygh said not to pick him up until three-thirty."

"Tygh?" I said, suddenly realizing where I'd seen this limousine before. It was on TV. It was a special about the Grammy Awards. . . .

"Told you I had connections," Zombie said.

"You . . . you work for Tygh Simpson, the lead singer of the Senseless Vultures?" I said, almost choking.

"And to think you called me a pimp. But I got no time to talk, kid! We gotta blow."

And once more we were whizzing away. Why was it that everyone I'd run into since leaving home drove so fast?

We careened onto the freeway. Then, on a whim, it seemed, Justin took an exit and we started climbing uphill. There were these fantastical buildings that sprouted out of the sheer rock. Then we were on this road called Mulholland Drive, which twists and spins along the top of a mountain, and I could see like this gigantic carpet of gridded light on either side, stretching on and on and on. It didn't seem like there was any end to this city at all. I was reeling from Justin's driving, but Zombie only laughed and said, "You should see it when teenagers use this strip for drag races." After a while I got into the swing of it and I was hollering wildly. I mean, like here I was, two thousand miles from home, taking a ride in Tygh Simpson's car! I wondered how I was going to prove it to anyone back home.

Home? What was I thinking?

I had a flash of memory—just a smell, really—the cake my mom had baked for my fourteenth birthday.

What an awesome cake that had been. No generic ingredients there. I had been standing at the top of the stairs and I caught a great big whiff of chocolate from the kitchen and it hit me all at once that in only two years I was going to be driving, and that meant I'd be able to go somewhere all by myself.

Without Ben . . .

Suddenly we were plunging downhill. I cried out and Zombie giggled. The road corkscrewed crazily and we emerged on an avenue lined with condominiums and palm trees. The street lights were yellow and harsh. Then there were all these restaurants with weird names like Casetta sul Prairie and Bangkok West . . . an empty park . . . a place that said it was a recording studio but looked more like a warehouse . . . some boarded-up buildings . . . an all-night grocery with a blinking, hot-pink neon portrait of a singing duck.

"This is sleazy," I said.

"Welcome to Burbank," Justin said.

He turned a corner and stopped the car. The street was called Damaris. It was quiet and dark. The only light came from another flashing neon sign in these like fake Oriental characters, this one electric blue. It said:

SUMIDAGAWA

and underneath it:

CROSSING THE RIVER OF OBLIVION

by appointment only

It was a very normal-looking suburban house, except for the sign. There was a front lawn with some miniature trees and unusually shaped large rocks that seemed to be illuminated from behind.

Justin said, "See you around." The door of the limousine popped open. "No souvenir hunting *please*," he added.

I paused. The house seemed so ordinary. Was this what I had come for? I heard Justin saying to Zombie, "I have to get you back home to Sherman Oaks and then I have to go to Stupendous Sound Systems to pick up Tygh, so let's get on with it."

"I thought you said you lived on the street," I said suspiciously to her. "You said you lived by—"

"Not everything the girl says is true," Justin said. "But some of it is. Sometimes she don't know what's real and what's not anymore. But you helped her, kid, by letting her do you a favor. That's the truth. See you around."

I got out of the car. It started. I saw it go down to the corner of Magnolia. I saw Zombie's face plastered to the rear window, looking wistfully back at me. I wondered what she was looking for.

I walked toward the house with the Jiffy Bag under my arm. The air was dry and hot. The sign winked on and off, on and off, as I reached the front steps.

There was a note tucked under the knocker with my name on it. I uncreased it. It said: "Key under third rock from left."

I went back to the lawn and peered at the rocks until I figured out where the key was. There was a note with it too. It said, "Back door."

I went around to the back of the house. There was a swimming pool and a gazebo. That was all I could see. One light was on in the back. I heard a siren in the distance. I unlocked the door and cautiously stepped inside.

I was in a kind of den or family room. A sofa bed

had been pulled down and made up with fresh-smelling sheets. The bedside light was on, and there was a note on the lampshade: "House call. Back at dawn. If hungry, food in refrigerator."

I went out into the hall, found the kitchen, and helped myself to a glass of milk and some cookies that were soft and had some kind of black jelly in them. The house was silent, shadowy, frightening. I tiptoed back to the other room.

I sat on the bed and looked around. There was a TV set with a VCR and a computer with a modem attached to it. The set was on but not showing anything but those dancing dots like on a blank videotape.

There was a remote control on the pillow. I was about to turn off the television when it burst into a familiar pattern of swirling colors—

"Ben!" I said softly.

HI, LITTLE BROTHER, flashed on the screen. **I'VE MISSED YOU.**

Then it turned itself off. I smiled. It must have been the first time since all this happened.

"I think I'll wait for Aunt Casey to come back," I thought, wondering what she meant by "house call." Was she a doctor too? I lay down on the bed. "Perhaps she can heal me of whatever it is I'm feeling. Perhaps she can take me across the river . . . wasn't that what Ben's message meant, that he was going to go on communicating with me even though he was dead? "When she comes, I'll have all the answers," I thought, "and then I'll be able to remember and I'll be able to feel everything, even the pain." I waited for only a few moments before I fell asleep.

CHAPTER 6

Séance at Lunch Break

I DREAMED I WAS back home by the bank of the Arkansas looking out at the cemetery by the light of the full moon. A voice called my name from across the water. There was a boat, and a man with a pole, wearing a kind of ninja costume. I kept hearing my name on the breeze. The air was tainted with the smell of blood and autumn leaves.

I couldn't see the ferryman's face because it was all wrapped up in a scarf. He handed me a candy bar.

I stepped from the boat. The wind was whispering among the cottonwoods. I saw my brother's gravestone. There was a voice coming from it: my name, over and over, the monotonous twang of a computer-generated voice.

Then the stone said, "Free me."

And I turned to the ferryman and took his sword from him and I slashed the gravestone in two with a single swing of the sword . . . the stone gave easily, cleanly, and there was nothing left.

And I said, "Is that what you want, Ben? Am I supposed to set you free?"

I must have said it out loud because I woke up with my own words still hanging in the air. It was so bright in the room that my eyes hurt. I must have slept a long time.

The phone was ringing.

I didn't reach it in time, because the modem picked up and then the TV screen winked on. I saw words beginning to form on the screen.

BY NOW YOU SHOULD BE GETTING USED TO YOUR NEW SURROUNDINGS, LITTLE BROTHER. YOU'VE PROBABLY ALREADY FOUND THE BOOK, BUT REALLY IT'S NOT MUCH OF A CLUE. TRUST AUNT CASEY. SHE MAY TELL YOU IT'S ALL ILLUSION, BUT THAT'S JUST TO THROW YOU OFF THE TRAIL.

I sprang up and darted across to the computer. But I couldn't make the machine say anymore. Had Ben really predicted my movements with incredible accuracy, or was he still alive somehow, reaching beyond the grave to contact me?

I didn't really like either of the two possibilities. But I had come to find out the truth, and I couldn't flinch away from it.

I looked around some more. There were some fresh clothes draped over a chair. The sizes were right, and Aunt Casey's taste was better than my mother's, I thought. At least I wouldn't die of embarrassment. I put on a shirt that made me look kind of like the captain of a spaceship, and these pants with star-shaped studs. I went into the bathroom to examine my new self, and I must say that I looked awesome. Then, remembering the guru's words, I took everything off and took a long, long shower.

I got dressed once again. My watch said twelve-thirty, and my stomach said I was starving. I didn't bother with shoes, but went barefoot into the kitchen. The door into the kitchen from the hallway outside

my room was open. There was another door on the far
side of the kitchen, which led to the rest of the house, I
presumed. It was shut, and, sitting in a chair like kind
of a sentinel, was that guru dude from the Far East
bookstore!

"What are *you* doing here?" I said.

"I might be saying same of you," he said in an
urgent whisper. "I live here."

"Live? But—"

"This is my postal address, though naturally, being
a seeker of the truth, I am also being a vagrant and
going from house to house begging for alms," he said.
"I am glad you have reached the place you were
looking for. I was worried you might not find it."

"You knew all the time—"

"I was knowing nothing. But by the same token I
am being surprised by nothing. All things flow together, all life is one, we are all linked by the great
wheel of karma. Or is it dharma? I can never get it
straight."

"Why are we whispering?" I whispered.

"Shhh! Must be monitoring séance now."

I had not been able to get a good look at the kitchen
last night because I just wanted to eat. But now I saw
that there was a TV screen, and like this mega-high-
tech console next to the microwave with flashing
lights and levers and knobs and buttons.

It was on the screen that I got my first view of Aunt
Casey. Oh, I knew I'd met her when I was a little kid,
but I didn't remember it. What I saw now wasn't
what I expected at all. It made my flesh creep.

On the screen, Aunt Casey was in the middle of
performing a séance. It was dark in the room on the
monitor, and the colors were muted. I saw a tiny
woman dressed in a Japanese kimono. Her features
were plastered with this whiteface, like clowns wear,

except on her it wasn't funny at all, it was ghostly.
Her lips were painted full and red, and her eyes had
been darkened. She was beautiful and terrifying at
the same time. I couldn't take my eyes off her.

"Interesting, isn't it, the way she is always combin-
ing East and West for maximum effect?" the guru
remarked, adjusting the monitor with a remote control with one hand while making a peanut butter and
jelly sandwich with the other. "East and West! That is
California for you."

Aunt Casey was sitting at one of those low tables
like you see in fancy Japanese restaurants. (I had
never been to one, but on those faraway satellite
channels you'll sometimes see a commercial for one.)
On either side of her there were people. The camera
was slightly overhead, facing Aunt Casey, and I
couldn't see all the way around the table. The people
were holding hands. I could see a man in a business
suit on one side and a woman wearing one of those
hats with feathers and fruit on top, like the Queen of
England.

"What are they doing?" I said.

The guru handed me the peanut butter and jelly
sandwich. I nibbled it distractedly. I was completely
under the spell of Aunt Casey's eyes. They seemed to
be looking straight at the camera, straight at me.

"Allow me to introduce myself," said the guru. "My
name is Raminder Hanuman Dass Chandragupta
Mahabhumi Rajan Bhajagovindam Ganesh Sujri-
dharma Mahesh Yogarishi Asvadeva."

"Radical!" I said. He was panting. "You got a
nickname?"

"Who is still saying *radical* nowadays?" the guru
said. "You must be from some remote outpost of this
great country, isn't it?" Before I could react, he said,
"Why were you not telling me you were looking for

your aunt? I would have driven you back myself."

"How was I to know? Everyone always seems to expect me to know everything," I said resentfully.

"Ah, but all things complete the cycle of being. But to be answering your question, my friends usually call me Jack. I am also, in certain circles, referred to as 'Hey, you.'"

I laughed. "But who are those dudes in there with Aunt Casey?" I asked him.

"That one—Mr. Zottoli. Studio executive. Very much money! The other—I am not sure. I think it is Caressa Byrd, author of such classics as *Desire's Diaphanous Dart*, and *Love's Leaping Lizard.*"

"You're having me on!" I said.

"I just made up the titles, but they are that sort of thing. Million-copy best-sellers. Personally I am sticking to science fiction, isn't it? But to continue: Mrs. Byrd is doing research for a new novel of hers, but Mr. Zottoli, ah, he is here for a very good reason. He is producing a film, and his partner has just died. He is hoping to get the partner's advice on choice of director, since the previous director is quitting."

"She's going to call up his spirit?" I said, so scared and excited by then that I could hardly contain myself. So this was why Ben sent me here! He did have something more to tell me. I pulled up a chair real close to the screen and kept my eyes glued to it, afraid I'd miss some vital clue. But this wasn't like some horror movie. There wasn't any of that bogus plunkety-plunk heart-thumping music, there weren't any body parts all over the floor, and we were sitting in a well-lit kitchen watching reality on a video monitor. And eating sandwiches.

First Aunt Casey started to hum in a quavery voice. Then she started shaking all over, and her voice grew deeper, deeper . . . and words began forming. Even though it was just a monitor screen, my knees were shaking against the chair leg.

"Do not be frightened," Jack the Guru said, handing me a glass of milk. "Time for special effects."

He came to the console and started pulling levers and adjusting knobs. Then this wailing noise filled the air . . . like the baying of wild coyotes in the moonlight. I jumped. Until I saw that he was shaping the sound with the aid of the console.

"Be helping me now," he said. "Push that button there a few times. Slowly."

I obeyed. As I watched the monitor, I saw the table start to levitate, and I heard a loud thwack, as though someone were stalking around the house with a bullwhip.

That Caressa Byrd lady was screaming, and Mr. Zottoli had sweat coming down his face. Awestruck, he whispered, "Is that really you, Mike? Is it?"

A man's voice issued from Aunt Casey's throat. "Brian," the voice said. "You should decide, not me. I can't decide for you anymore. This is your time."

"But it was our project," the executive said. "I hate to think of you cut out of the deal like this. . . ."

"I go toward the light now, Brian. Don't worry about me," came that masculine voice from the lips of the tiny woman.

The executive was actually crying. He said, sobbing, "Thanks, Mike. Thanks for setting me free."

"More sound effects," Jack said, playing the console like a synthesizer keyboard, flooding the room with ghostly music. "And you, push the button on the far left. That will be bringing back on house lights."

I did so.

The lights were harsh in the room on the monitor screen, and Mr. Zottoli looked tired, like he hadn't slept. The tears were running down his furrowed cheeks.

I heard my aunt's "normal" voice now: "You must not be sad, Mr. Zottoli. Weeping is cleansing, but when it is done, life must go on." She smiled at him.

The other woman, the writer, said, "Well, it's been most fascinating to see you work." She was writing out a check.

"Please excuse me," Aunt Casey said. "I have something that must be attended to now. It is something I fear I have neglected."

She rose from the table, daintily adjusted her kimono, and walked out of range of the TV camera.

Moments later I heard a light tapping on the door from the kitchen to the front of the house. Guru Jack opened it quickly and closed it again. One minute she was on television, the next she was there in the kitchen. She seemed even smaller than before, and fragile as a porcelain doll. I couldn't tell how old she was, although I thought she must be a few years older than my parents. She was wiping the white makeup from her face with a damp rag.

"You're here," she said to me, as though I had just come in from down the block.

"Aunt Casey—" I began. And then like all these words came tumbling out, more anger than I knew I had in me: "It's all a fraud, it's all phony in there —it's all these high-tech machines and sound effects —you're a fake! I don't know why Ben made me come here, I don't know what he's trying to tell me!" I brought my hand smashing down on the console, but Guru Jack stopped me and gripped me. I tried to wrest my arms free, but he sure knew some powerful wrestling holds for a peace-and-love kind of dude.

"You're just a fake, a fake, a fake!" I shouted, not

caring if the people in the other room heard me. "I thought I could reach Ben through you, and I was wrong. I'll never reach him now."

"Jeremiah," Aunt Casey said. Somehow, the way she said it, it didn't sound like she was making fun of me. There was something of Ben in the way she said my name, and I found that I couldn't get mad about it. "J.J. The last time I saw you, you were just a toddler. You were yelling your heart out because Santa didn't bring you the right dinosaur, remember that?"

I did, suddenly, after more than ten years. My uncle and his new wife had been staying with us that Christmas. When she said that, she seemed to put my whole life in perspective, and I knew that she was not my enemy. Somehow the idea that she had held that memory for ten years, like, in trust for me, like she was some kind of safety-deposit box in the bank, touched me more than I could explain. I wanted to trust her, I really did. But I didn't understand how she could claim that a bunch of sci-fi effects made her into a real medium who could communicate with the dead. It didn't click.

"You're so full of so many feelings, you don't know who to love or hate, or why," she said softly. "But look into the monitor, look at the face of that man. See his grief. You think that is fraud, that feeling in his face?"

"But you tricked him," I said.

"Medium's art is art of illusions," she said. "But core is truth."

"That's just a line you're giving me," I said, not wanting to give up my anger yet.

"That man, his friend died in car crash. They were producing movie together. But you see, all this time he really wanted it all to himself, he wanted his friend gone, you see? And he was angry at himself for wanting it, but he couldn't help himself. Today I help him see that he must not feel guilt anymore."

I couldn't really grasp it. It was like when Mrs. Hulan tried to explain one of the finer points of English grammar in class and no one could see what difference it made.

Then I stared at the man's face on the TV screen again, and I saw not just TV grief, but something deeper too, I think. "What are you trying to tell me? That you're a real medium, that all this hardware is just window dressing?"

"The medium does not reach out to the spirits of the dead by herself. There has to be something else —something in the heart of the person who asks. They say I am a good medium, but I can do nothing without the thing in the heart. The other stuff, the window dressing, that is for the ones who need it. What is in your heart, J.J. Madigan?"

I knew the answer to that. What was in my heart was the empty place, the void. The dark pit where memory dared not reach.

She came close to me. I stood taller than her, even though she was a grown-up. But there was authority in her eyes, and there was this total calm inside them, like the surface of the river on a windless summer day.

"Why did he have to die?" I said at last, feeling a sliver slip loose from the secret place inside me.

"Did you think I would give you the answer to that? How could I know such answers? They are great mysteries that philosophers have argued for thousand thousand years."

"That's what I was sent here to find out, wasn't it?"

"I don't know," she said, shrugging. "You loved him very much. I did too. He was my favorite nephew. But not the same thing as you, because you were with him all the time, you breathed each other's air, lived each other's life maybe."

"Can you really help me to talk to the dead?"

"What I do is always the same. All life is an illusion, therefore perhaps death is too. You see the séance on the screen. For some it is deception, for others it is miracle. Which one it is depends on"—she tapped her chest lightly with her fist—"what is in your heart."

CHAPTER 7

A High-Tech Medium

"WELL," MY AUNT said, looking me over, "you want to eat?"

"Uh, I guess." I just couldn't get over the whole thing. I just kept staring at Aunt Casey. She was totally beautiful even if she was probably older than my parents. I mean not beautiful like the faces in a rock video but like the cottonwoods that ringed the graveyard across the river.

"I have been feeding the boy peanut butter and jelly sandwiches," Jack the Guru said. "He seems to be responding well. But he has much anger. He is angry because of his brother's death, no? And also angry because he thinks he has discovered falsehood, fraud . . . and the young are having such a powerful sense of justice, isn't it? But perhaps he is also angry at himself, because he feels he does not have enough sadness."

"Like what are you talking about, dude?" I turned to him in amazement. "You can't just open me up and read me like one of those books in your store. You don't know anything about me yet." I realized as I spoke to him that I *was* getting angry. That made me uneasy. I don't like to give away anything about

myself and it's even worse when people start analyz-
ing me.

"On the contrary," Jack said, between mouthfuls of
peanut butter, "I am not seeing what is within your
heart at all."

Aunt Casey said, "For God's sake, let's give him real
food." She started to shove all the computer equipment, the tangled wires and black boxes, to one
corner of the kitchen counter. Then she opened the
refrigerator and pulled out some kind of red meat.
"You like raw tuna?" she said. "That was your Uncle
Elbert's favorite, you know."

"It was?" I had heard of sushi, of course—they
always showed dudes wolfing it down in those ninja
movies—but I was kind of unprepared to watch
someone standing around a suburban kitchen in a
kimono, slicing a humongous slab of bright red raw
fish. I watched her making these paper-thin petals
and painstakingly arranging them until they looked
like roses, and then she made stems from pieces of
cucumber.

Maybe the guru thought I was full of all this
resentment and rage. But I was too fascinated by
what Aunt Casey was doing to think of anything else
right now. She was carving that tuna with so much, I
don't know, tenderness or love or something. "Why
do you do all that work?" I said. "I mean, like it's
going to get eaten anyway."

"Just because it only lasts for a short time," she
said softly, "doesn't mean it doesn't have the right to
be as beautiful as it can be."

The way she said that made me think of my brother. He'd only lasted a short time, hadn't he? But he'd
planned everything so intricately. Like slicing the
tuna and turning it into flowers.

"Try it," Aunt Casey said, giving me a pair of

chopsticks and pouring a little dish of soy sauce for me. I did. It wasn't that bad, once you got over the gag reflex. After a couple more bites I realized it was good and I said so. She said, "You see, it's the art of illusion at work again. A hunk of raw fish is a rose is a rose."

I said, "I don't see what this has to do with Ben. I don't see why I was supposed to come here. I think maybe I should go home."

"Sure, J.J.," she said. "It is entirely up to you. But you are always welcome here."

I tried to work up another one of my bad moods, but it was too difficult. She was so calm all the time. If I were to throw a fit, it would look pretty retarded.

I thought about going home too, and then I remembered the drive to the funeral and the fight over the chickens . . . and watching the burial from the other side of the river. I realized I just couldn't go home, not yet. Maybe I wasn't going to get the answers I wanted or envisioned, but there had to be some kind of answers here, there just had to be.

"I guess I'm staying," I said at last.

"In that case," Aunt Casey said, "might as well put you to work. Everyone else who drifts through my house ends up working."

"Working?" I asked, bewildered.

"On the show," she said.

"The grand illusion," Guru Jack said.

"The summoning of the dead," my aunt said.

The thought sent chills up my spine. "What can I do?" I said, knowing full well that part of what I'd seen was trickery, but knowing too that there was something else to all this, something both exciting and totally terrifying. "I just can't," I said. "I mean, with my brother . . . I mean . . ."

I was afraid, really afraid. But I hated to admit . . . I wanted it too, I wanted it real bad. There were those messages in the computer, so maybe there was some kind of hidden truth behind the high-tech deception.

I wanted so much for Ben not to be dead, to be able to touch some part of him, even a shadow, even an illusion.

"So what do I do?" I said.

"I'll show you after lunch," Aunt Casey said.

I had a few more pieces of raw fish, and then my education in the art of spiritualism began.

Anyways, if you are someone who wants to contact a dead person, and you come to Aunt Casey's, you will see some pretty uncanny stuff. If you don't know how any of it's done, this is the kind of thing you'll experience:

First, you go into this big like Oriental living room with the low table. There are these big screens made of bamboo and rice paper that surround the room. One of the partitions can be drawn back to reveal a humongous statue of like this Buddha dude, except, Aunt Casey will explain, it's really some minor deity with an unpronounceable name. There's all this incense and there's no air-conditioning, so the air is all clouded up and heavy with a smell of burning flowers. You hear eerie music: high-pitched flute music and this jangling, twanging Japanese stringed instrument called a *samisen*. Also there's a deep drum and another percussion instrument, a hollow-sounding tap-tap-tapping.

You'll be asked to sit down and Aunt Casey explains, slowly and carefully, about the ceremony. There isn't really any "mysteries of the East" kind of thing at all, she says, because it's the same way of talking to the dead that gypsies and people like that have been using for thousands of years. "I'm going to go into a trance," she says, "and then another person will appear—a spirit guide. He doesn't have a name. I just call him the Ferryman."

She goes on to tell the ancient Japanese tale of Sumidagawa, Curlew River, which I've already talked about, in bits and pieces. By now you're getting into the swing of it, you're getting kind of spooked by the music and the incense.

Everyone holds hands around the table. The lights dim. The music gets louder. You get scared, maybe. But you think about the dead person. Maybe it's a relative. Often it's a friend and you feel there was something you left unsaid, something that will torment you until it gets spoken. That's why you overcame your disbelief and came here in the first place. Because of how strong your feelings for this dead person are.

Aunt Casey drifts off. Her eyes kind of glaze over, or sometimes they are tightly shut. You hear an ominous thumping. Did the table move, or are you just imagining things? Your heart beats faster and faster and you want to run maybe but still there's whatever it was you came for, the thing you need to say, and it keeps you sitting there, clutching your neighbor's hand in fear and hope.

Then there's another voice coming from Aunt Casey's throat: a gruff voice with a real heavy accent, like a bad guy in a samurai movie. It's the Ferryman. The voice is totally hypnotic because it's coming from the throat of this tiny woman. You can't move. And the voice says something like, "I've come to lead you across the river. You already know who you have come to meet. I can only guide you. I cannot tell you if your friend will come to you. The river flows toward a mighty light, and the dead will not be held back forever."

Sometimes a second voice chimes in. It seems to

come from the great statue, and it's high-pitched and terribly distant. Maybe it's the voice of someone you know.

At last, one by one, the departed ones speak to you. At times it's through Aunt Casey, at times through the great idol itself. Sometimes it's the one you came to find. Sometimes it's someone else. We make no guarantees here; you cross the river at your own risk. They speak in their own voices—at least, it seems that way to you—every inflection, every quirk, every familiar expression. It's uncanny. It chills you. You're scared, terribly scared, but somehow you also feel cleansed and purified. By the time the lights come back on, you're probably in tears. Shaken, anyway. And you believe. For a while at least.

"But," Aunt Casey told me, "the things we do for that illusion sometimes make us cynical."

"Do you believe in ghosts?" I asked her as I helped her with the dishes. "I mean, when you're so busy manipulating what other people see—"

"Does it matter if I believe or not?" she said. "I never thought about that."

"Sure you did," I said. "You must have."

"Never anymore," she said.

And she led me into the great big Oriental living room I've been talking about, which until that moment I'd only seen on a television screen.

"Got to be getting back to the store now," Guru Jack's voice came from the kitchen.

"See you later," I said.

Then I looked around and caught my breath.

In the first place, seeing the room on screen and imagining it from Aunt Casey's description weren't anything like the reality. I guess nothing could be as awesome as what I'd seen in my mind's eye. But the room seemed small, cramped almost.

The most impressive thing was the big statue. "That thing is humongous!" I said.

"Yes," Aunt Casey said, "it controls some of the lighting and sometimes the second voice."

It even had clothes on, these flowing robes kind of like what Guru Jack wore. Aunt Casey led me behind it, and there was a door in its back. If you pushed this button, it swung open and you could crawl inside. She motioned me to do just that and I did.

I had to squirm a bit, and at first I thought I wasn't going to be able to breathe. Anyone bigger than me would probably have suffocated.

The inside of the statue was roomier than I expected. It was hot and sounds were muffled. If I leaned back, I could stick my legs deep into the cavity and stretch out a bit on this padded area, and I could look ahead and see out of a slit in the statue's chest. It was covered over with thin cloth, muslin I think, so no one would suspect that it concealed a peeping tom. There was also a computer keyboard and a flat-screen monitor.

The monitor was flashing my name over and over.

I hit a key and the flashing stopped. Instead there was another message: BET YOU HAVEN'T THOUGHT ABOUT ME ALL DAY, LITTLE BROTHER.

THAT'S A LIE! I typed. How long was this going to go on?

I TAKE IT YOU'RE INSIDE THE STATUE NOW. I FIGURED YOU'D GET TO IT SOONER OR LATER, the computer said. LONELY, ISN'T IT? CUT OFF, TOTALLY CUT OFF. YOU CAN BARE-LY HEAR THE WORLD OUTSIDE. BUT IF YOU LISTEN CAREFULLY, OH SO CAREFULLY, YOU

CAN HEAR THE SOUND OF THE RIVER.
I closed my eyes and listened hard. And oh, I heard it. Maybe it was just the blood rushing through my head. Against the silence it was a torrent. I tried to imagine being dead. It must be a terrible thing. Like being trapped in the belly of this idol and never being able to come out.

I thought I heard Ben's voice.

I cried out. My cry was magnified somehow; it started to echo. Some electronic distorting device inside the statue was picking it up and turning it into something fierce and resonant.

There was no answer. Only the sound of water. When I opened my eyes, I saw another message on the screen:

WHEN YOU'RE STUCK IN A PLACE LIKE THIS, LITTLE BROTHER, SOMETIMES YOU START TO IMAGINE THINGS.

"Let me out!" I shouted, pounding on the wall of the statue. Everything seemed to be closing in on me, and the murmur of the river became a roar. I couldn't hear myself screaming. My fists were chafing on the metal lining. Suddenly I felt the surface behind me give way and I started to slide out. I flailed, trying to grab on to something.

Then Aunt Casey was holding on to me. I guess I must have been pretty hysterical.

"The voice," she said. "It is very effective, no?"

"Scared the living daylights out of me."

She laughed.

"It's not funny," I said.

She said, "If it scares you, it will surely work on the customers."

"But I don't want to be scared. I didn't come here to . . . I mean, I was hoping that you'd do something to take away my being scared. Isn't that what Ben wanted?" But I wasn't at all sure of that. When I closed my eyes and tried to conjure up my brother's face, I couldn't see it for a moment. I only saw one of those masks in that book of Japanese plays.

All she said was, "It is good to be frightened. We play with fire. We should not lose our fear of it. There is nothing rational about calling up the dead. But it's more exciting than selling insurance. That's what your Uncle Elbert wanted me to get into."

I had to laugh when she said that. I laughed hard, really hard. I was totally helpless with laughter. I guess when you can't take it anymore, laughing is all you can do.

Aunt Casey gave me a big hug and said, "You will be a wonderful assistant, I know it. It's all much more effective if I have someone inside and I don't have to rely on Jack in the kitchen for everything."

This was just incredible. I mean, I had journeyed all this distance . . . to get a job as this assistant rattle-shaker for this voodoo ceremony! And I was ready to believe there was something to it! "Burbank, the Emerald City," I managed to blurt out between fits of laughing. "You and me running the whole show with high-tech special effects. This is baaad!"

"So you'll take the job?"

"How will I know what to say? With the voice, I mean."

"If you have the talent, it will come naturally. Your brother had the talent very much, you know. Many people were interested in him."

I stopped laughing. "Are you talking about that Webb Foundation, or whatever it was?" I said, thinking of the letter from them I'd found, and of Ben and the telepathy cards, and of how he seemed to be able to predict the future. "I can't do any of that stuff."

"I think you may have it inside you. Just close your

eyes and think of the river."

"Sure, what the hell." In the back of my mind, behind the laughter, I knew that it would take me one step nearer the Forgetting Place.

I climbed back inside the idol. The screen had switched to a Senseless Vultures video. In the LCD flat screen the Vultures seemed totally alien. There was no music. All I could hear was the river raging. I felt powerless against the current. But I knew the river would carry me where I needed to go.

CHAPTER 8

Nightmares

THERE WAS SOMETHING timeless about Aunt Casey's house. It wasn't just that people seemed to come and go at weird hours all the time, or that you could always find ancient and brand-new things lying side by side all over the place. It was partly Aunt Casey herself. It was partly the business we were in, because the people who came to us were people who wanted time to reverse itself or to stand still. For the next few days I took up my post in the big statue and watched through the slit in its belly. I didn't go into any trances and I didn't start spouting mysterious words of wisdom. But then, I had no reason to believe that I had "the talent," as Aunt Casey called it.

I was starting to believe in "the talent," though. For one thing, what Aunt Casey said and did really did seem to touch people where it counted. And I couldn't figure out how she did it sometimes. Oh, the flashing lights and the sound effects, I got all that the first day, but not those uncanny insights.

The other thing was that those modem messages kept coming from my dead brother. And they always seemed so accurate.

I was almost starting to feel better now. I think that

maybe I thought of my grief as kind of a sickness. I felt I was getting closer and closer to a cure. Time would come when I'd understand everything, then I could snip away the suffering and I'd go home and everything would be all right again.

Everything was cool except for the dreams. The dream of the river crossing came back every night, and it was more vivid every time.

It got so I didn't want to go to sleep. So I'd just lie there staring at the TV screen. Sometimes I'd put it on MTV and turn the sound off and let the images wash through my mind. Sometimes it was a late-night horror show. Other times I'd pick a station that was off the air and just gaze into the snow, trying to keep awake.

One night—the third or fourth night, I guess—I was doing just that. The snow danced on the screen. Everything else in the room was dark. I guess I was hypnotized by the flickering light. I wasn't asleep and I wasn't awake. Sometimes when you stare at random patterns long enough, you can see things. I mean, I always felt that way about the shadows in the closet in my room at home. The shadows would shift and suddenly there'd be a face there, or maybe the outline of a monstrous figure. If I looked away, it would disappear after a while. When I was about eight years old, Ben showed me how you could tough it out. You'd stare it down, and repeat, over and over, "You're just a shadow." If I stared at it real hard, it would usually turn into something else. It wouldn't be scary anymore.

It usually happened with the closet but it could also happen with a television set, after they played the national anthem and there was nothing left but fuzz and hissing.

It was starting to happen now. I could see something—a face—all ripped up, covered with blood.

"I'm not going to get scared," I told myself.

And I gazed at it, not even blinking, willing it to go away. But it wouldn't. And when I closed my eyes, it was still there, a ghostly afterimage, like burned into my brain.

And I heard a voice: "I'll see you again in the Forgetting Place."

"I don't want to go," I said. "I'm not ready." I thought I must be going crazy.

My eyes were still squeezed tight. I felt a hand clutch my hand . . . not quite real . . . and terribly cold. Pulling me from the bed. A whispering voice: "We're going to cross together. You and me. You're not going to let a little thing like death separate us, are you? I mean, you were always like my shadow, my other self. I need you."

I could feel the sweat slick on my cheeks and throat. Cold, totally cold. "If the Forgetting Place is so great," I said, "why do I feel so terrible about it?"

"Listen to the cry of the curlew."

I could hear the faint alien music that Aunt Casey used to accompany her séances.

"I don't think the Forgetting Place is like Nirvana at all," I said angrily. "I think it's where the pain is. And I don't want to go there." But I was being dragged, kicking and screaming, onto this wooden boat that loomed up out of the fog.

My brother was wearing these long robes and was pushing the boat with a gnarled pole. He didn't look back at me. He just kept looking at the far bank, where the cottonwoods poked from the mist . . . I could feel the boat rocking and the water churning, but the land was always out of reach, and my face was damp from the slimy touch of the fog. . . . "Stop," I said weakly. "Stop."

"But you always go where I go," said Ben's voice, daring me. Then he pulled out a pack of those psychic research cards and tossed them at me. I looked at them.

"Star," he said, without turning back. It was right. I shuffled the cards and pulled out another one. "Rectangle."

I could see gravestones wrapped in ribbons of mist. I could almost read the inscriptions. But the river was like those corridors in your dreams where you keep running and running and you never get there.

"Ben, let's go back to the house." I turned up a card.

"Can't. Wiggly parallel lines."

"Let's go to Mr. Miles's place. Why don't you borrow the car and we can drive down to Lamar? Why don't you—"

"Come on, little brother, let me have some fun for a change! I'm tired of humoring you. Smiley face. Star. Square."

"Okay." I felt like a little boy all of a sudden. Ben was the only person who could ever make me feel that way. I was sure it was him, even though he was dressed in these dark robes. He had like this black hood over his face, like one of those monk dudes in the Middle Ages. I went on turning up the cards and he went on calling them. "What harm could it do?" I was thinking. "This is a dream, only a dream."

"Listen then. Star. Star. Star."

"Yeah." I was dropping them, one by one, into the water, watching them float away. . . .

"The place I'm taking you, it's quiet and full of light and you never have to worry about anything again

. . . not about the past and not about the present and not about the future. It's totally calm, little brother. And you'll forget everything. Everything. And nothing will hurt anymore. Those wiggly lines again."

But I didn't want to go with him. And I didn't want to tell him that. I tried to but the words just wouldn't come. Because as always I wanted to be just like him. If I didn't go to this place, maybe he would think I didn't care about him anymore. It wasn't fair that he would put me in this bind. I struggled to say something but my tongue was stuck and I couldn't open my mouth, and finally I was so frustrated I started to pound at him with my fists. But there was no flesh underneath the robes. Only bones, brittle bones that creaked and tinkled when I struck them. "For God's sake, at least look at me," I said.

He continued to punt, straining against the pole. His hands were withered and skeletal. I reached up and tore at his hood. He turned to me. It was my brother, it really was. He was smiling. Like nothing had happened. I had one card left in my hand.

"Ben!" I cried out. "It was just a trick, one of your illusions." I turned the card faceup, smiling—

But the card showed Death with a hooded face and a skull and a scythe and coal-red burning eyes. I tried to throw it away but it was like glued to my hand. "You cheated!" I was shouting. "This isn't one of the cards!" Even in the dream I knew that Death was a card in the tarot deck, which is used for fortune-telling, not for psychic guessing games.

"Death," my brother said softly. With so much longing in his voice! I stared at his face, with his funny half smile and his gaze fixed on some point far away, in the cemetery across the water—

But the face started to melt and there was only the skull beneath and the card was a skull too and the card was Death and I started to scream and scream and scream. . . .

And I felt Aunt Casey's arms around me as I woke. It must have been long past midnight. The TV was still hissing and snowing. I suddenly realized I was still screaming and I stopped myself. I could hear this strangled sound coming from my own throat, but it felt like a stranger's voice.

"It's all right," she said softly. And she hugged me real hard to her. I remember thinking that, all through those days of tragedy, this was the first time someone had touched me, come close to me.

"I was scared," I said.

"You were dreaming maybe," she said.

"How can a dream feel so . . . so real?" I wanted to thank her for holding me like that, but I didn't say anything because I didn't want her to think I was a little kid or something. I only said, "I saw him, I think."

"Yes."

"He wants me to go too."

"Where?"

"The Forgetting Place."

Aunt Casey smiled. I didn't understand why. "He always had his own name for everything," she said. And that was strange, because I had always thought I was the only person who knew that about my brother. "She must have memories of him," I thought, "that I'll never know about, maybe." And I was disturbed at that.

"You want to eat?" she said abruptly.

I nodded. Maybe food would take my mind off the dream.

We went into the kitchen. "You want raw fish?" she asked me.

"Sure, I guess."

"Personally, I will have microwave pizza."

I let out a nervous laugh. "Me too, I guess."
She stood on tiptoe to look into the freezer. "Only
one left. Raw fish for you. Better for you anyway. Junk
food for old people—vitamins no use anyway."

"You're not old!"

"Sit down."

We didn't talk for a while as she made food. She
didn't turn on any lights, but the moon was big and
full and the whole kitchen glowed with a pale blue
light.

At last she said, "Do you miss him?"

"Of course I do!" I said almost defiantly. "He's—" I
couldn't begin to tell her all he had meant to me.

"You want to cry?" she said softly. "I won't look.
It's okay."

"I just can't," I said.

"Ah, you are angry too."

"I guess." But I didn't really know what she meant.

"I miss him too," she said.

"But you hardly ever saw him!" I said.

"You see what I mean? You *are* angry, so angry. You
want the grief all to yourself. Because it's *yours* and
no one else's. Your grief is like a great big wad of
money and you think you can hoard it in the bank and
never spend it and it'll keep earning interest until you
hit a million bucks and you can retire. But grief isn't
something you can be selfish with. You have to spend
it, you have to share it."

She spoke very gently to me, and I guess she meant
well, but I didn't feel like another dose of philosophiz-
ing. "You sound just like him," I said. I tried to keep
the resentment out of my voice—I mean, she was
putting me up, and putting up with me, and all—but
I think it showed anyway. I'd been clumsily stabbing

at this piece of raw fish with my chopsticks, and now it slithered onto the floor. I just sat there watching it. In the moonlight it had an odd sheen, like that junky titanium jewelry they sell in novelty stores.

"How did you feel when you started getting computer messages?" Aunt Casey said.

"Totally spooked. Especially about that 'meeting me in the Forgetting Place' business."

"What do you think he meant by that?"

"Once he told me it means Nirvana . . . the place where everything is still. But to me it's something else . . . it's like a black hole . . . where I've stashed those memories so that they can't ever come out again . . . and I don't ever want to go there. But he wants me to."

"How will you get there?"

"In the dream, I almost reach the other side of the river. But never all the way."

"Why do you think he killed himself?"

"I don't know," I said. I must have been shouting, because she kind of shrank back. "Do you know?" I said, daring her almost. "He always used to call you, didn't he? Didn't he call you up on the very day he—" I stopped. I realized I was acting like it was her fault or something. Well, maybe it was. It sure as hell wasn't mine. It couldn't be. Could it?

She said, "I'm as much in the dark as you. He was talking about this, I think, Webb Foundation."

"What do they do?" I had this vision of mad scientists clustering around my brother, observing, observing, observing. Electrodes attached to his head, and the scientists turning up cards endlessly, mechanically.

"They want to know the future. They are always looking for people who can see it very clearly, you know what I mean?"

"Like Ben?"

"Your brother had the talent, all right."

"I don't understand why it would make him—"

"I don't either."

Abruptly she got up. "Have to go."

"What? It's three in the morning or something."

"House call."

"That's what your note said, when I came here. But on your answering machine it says you never make house calls."

"Few can afford."

"Another movie producer maybe?" I said.

"Maybe. Go to bed."

"And tomorrow? Who do you have lined up for tomorrow's show?"

"Tomorrow you're going into town with Guru Jack. All this talk of spiritualism is getting to you. You watch enough séances, you start believing everything. You need a dose of the real world—"

I laughed. "That bookstore is the real world?"

"All is illusion."

She smiled again, that quirky smile that reminded me of Ben at his most frustrating. There was nothing I could say to her, so I went back to the bedroom. Later I heard her car pull out.

Suddenly, as I was drifting off into sleep for the second time that night, the television clicked on. It was one of those test patterns. It had the profile of an Indian with a war bonnet in the middle. "It must be almost morning," I thought.

Then the Indian kind of blinked out, pixel by pixel, and there was a new image in its place. The skull. The card of Death. The hooded figure, stooped, swinging his scythe in jerky computer animation . . . like in a low-budget cartoon. You can make pictures move that way with a home computer and a good graphics program. So I knew the pictures came from Ben.

And words flashed across the screen:

NIGHTMARES GETTING YOU DOWN, LITTLE BROTHER?

I'M SORRY, SO SORRY.

DOES THIS CARD LOOK FAMILIAR?

I'M SORRY, SO SORRY.

I'M NOT DOING THIS TO HURT YOU, HONEST I'M NOT.

I got out of bed and tried to turn off the set but nothing happened. Then I ripped the pillowcase off my bottom pillow and hung it over the set. I looked around for something to hold it down with. I found an ashtray and a bronze Buddha image.

"He can't know all this," I thought. "It's got to be a trick."

But I really wanted to believe there was someone on the other side of the river, calling for me from the country of mist and shadows.

"It's a trick!" I told myself over and over.

CHAPTER 9

A Day With Guru Jack

JACK WAS ALREADY waiting for me when I finished breakfast. Aunt Casey was nowhere to be seen; probably she was in bed, what with the late-night house call.

"Today I am being baby-sitter, isn't it?" he said, as he carefully twirled a fold of his robe and tucked it under his armpit just so. "We will have fun."

I gathered up all Ben's treasures—the CD Walkman and the contents of the Jiffy Bag—and put on the headphones. I strutted out the door to the strains of "Doggie Come a-Gawking," the last cut on the Vultures album. I noticed that the Guru too was wearing headphones, and that the wires led down his neck and into the robe. "What are you listening to?" I said.

We traded headphones. I was practically deafened by this wailing woman and these twanging sounds and this drum pounding away. "What *is* that noise?" I said. "It sounds like a wolverine being run over by an eighteen-wheeler."

"That is quite correct," he said.

"Give me back my Vultures!" I said, laughing.

"No, the store first," he said.

I realized he couldn't hear a word I was saying, and

hadn't mastered the lip-reading skills that are like totally essential for anyone who's plugged in a lot. So I just yanked the phones off his head. "You don't like Indian music?" he said. "Very restful, you know."

I put the Vultures back on and turned the volume way up.

The guru's convertible was, I mean, radical. It seemed to have been put together from bits and pieces of other cars. There was a Rolls-Royce hood ornament. It seemed out of place beside the fins and teeth and the swirly patterns that were painted in garish colors all over the hood. I gaped. It was like something from my parents' photo album with the shots of the old commune, the ancient times when they had, you know, hippies and stuff. "Can this thing actually, you know, *go* anywhere?" I shouted.

"Oh, you like it? I built it myself from spare parts from my cousin Raminder's junkyard." He beamed and waved wildly at the car. "Hop in. You will soon be enjoying my natural air-conditioning."

"Great," I said. It wasn't noon yet, but the sun was hot today. I climbed in—literally, since the door on the passenger side was jammed—and sat down.

Like everyone else I'd encountered since running away from home, the guru drove like a demon. I could see what he meant by natural air-conditioning.

"You missed the freeway!" I shouted as we zoomed right past the exit.

"Today we are taking surface streets, isn't it?" Guru Jack said, nodding vigorously. "Let me show you some of the sights of North Hollywood." He took his hands off the steering wheel and started pointing things out to me. "Over here, Mr. Donut. Over there, a magnificent Burger King." He was driving too fast for me to notice. I started laughing because the hot wind on my face was messing up my hair and making it tickle my neck. "What lies at the bottom of the ocean and shakes? A nervous wreck," the guru said in his most awe-inspiring voice. I started cracking up again. "So you have heard the joke about the city carrot and the country carrot?" he said.

"He will remain a vegetable all his life," I said, quoting the infamous punch line.

"But the part in between is so very funny, isn't it?" as we careened across the boulevard and streaked onto a street bordered with palm trees. A pedestrian started to cuss us out. "A little old lady," Guru Jack said, chuckling. "That is coming to a hundred and fifty points, no?"

"No!" I shouted. "Only if you run them over."

"Too late now. Anyway, it is the thought that counts, isn't it?"

I started screaming with laughter again. Guru Jack put his arm over my shoulder and said, "It is good for you to laugh."

Suddenly I felt like I didn't have any right to laugh anymore. Jack didn't say anything but I knew he knew and it was awful because I realized he cared about my feelings.

But he only said, "Enough surface streets. Let's take the freeway." And we were off again.

Back in the store, I sat in that sort of meditating place with all the floor cushions while Jack minded the cash register. I put the headphones back on and opened up the Sumidagawa book, trying to puzzle it out again. It seemed pretty boring. There were these long speeches in poetry, kind of like Shakespeare. I flipped through to the end, where there was a bunch of illustrations. There were photographs of these masks that used to be worn in Noh plays, alien-looking things. Some had lightning jags across the faces, some had fuzzy shocks of hair, almost like punks. But the one that showed the madwoman—the main character in *Sumidagawa*—was real simple. The lips were half parted as though she were about to say something. I wondered if she had something to say to me, some secret.

Her eyes were empty, of course, because it was just a mask. I stared into those vacant sockets for a long time.

No one came into the store all morning. At least, I didn't hear the door chime. I remembered that the first time I was here there was this dude dressed as a ninja standing outside who was supposed to drum up business. I guess he didn't work mornings.

At last I heard something. It was Jack's robe rustling against the straw matting. "You are wanting drink?" he said, holding out a can of soda. He saw what I was looking at. "Yes, it is a very beautiful mask, isn't it? It has grief and joy at the same time, you know. And madness and sanity." He had a big bag of french fries in his other hand and offered me some.

"I don't see how it can be both sad and happy." I smiled and took the drink from him. "I guess I'm not really getting enough use out of the book," I said. "I feel kind of embarrassed you gave it to me."

"I will not mind if you give it back. Who knows, someone may want it." I handed it to him and I saw him put it back on the shelf.

"You know anything about the Webb Foundation?" I asked him out of the blue.

"Yes, a little. They contacted me once. Your aunt too."

"What do they do? I mean . . . they were *testing* Ben. I think. Yeah, testing him."

"They have this plan for seeing into the future.

They think, every psychic can see a little way . . . why not be establishing a vast network of psychics and all concentrate at once? Someone once said, if every single person in the world would concentrate hard at the same time, they could be generating enough psychic energy to lift the Great Pyramid an inch or two. Sounds like nonsense? It probably is. But they wanted to be using the same principle . . . they are saying, everyone can see into the future a little bit. A talented person can see quite a lot, but still it is like squinting right up against the wrong side of a one-way mirror, isn't it?"

"So they were going to get a whole bunch of psychics to look into the future at once . . . and maybe it would all become clear?"

"Yes. Front-page *National Enquirer* kind of thing. Big stuff."

I wondered why Ben would get involved with people like that. But he *did* have talent. How else had he known that Mr. Miles's wife was going to die? And those computer messages that kept coming, each one seeming to know exactly what I had done that day. Maybe it was him reaching out from beyond the grave. But maybe it was all stuff he'd seen already, before he died.

Was *that* what had made him kill himself? Something he had seen? But nothing in the world could be that bad. . . .

"When were they going to have the big psychic linkup?" I said.

"I think, I am not knowing, it was supposed to happen a week or two ago."

I knew I had something at last. It wasn't much of a clue, but it was a thing I could grasp at.

Guru Jack said, "I hope you are not believing in all that nonsense, though. None of this has ever been proved, and for every fantastical explanation there is almost always a logical one also, if you are searching for one and not jumping to conclusions. . . ."

"So you don't believe you can foretell the future."

"A future, maybe. But I do not think . . . *the* future. There are existing millions and millions of possible futures, universes upon universes. How can one of them be *the* future?"

"But—" I didn't want to believe him. I guess I wanted a way to have certainty. He wasn't offering me any hope. "What's the scientific rationale for tarot cards?" I said, remembering the card halves taped together in my Jiffy Bag. I pulled them out and showed them to him.

"Some people think, the fortune-teller feels what's going to happen because his mind takes in all those details that other people miss . . . unconsciously, as he shuffles and reshuffles the deck he knows so well, he manages to put them into the order that will reveal the future he sees. Sort of like a dealer cheating at poker, only all beneath the threshold of consciousness."

"Awesome! Can people really do that?"

"It's a theory. But why are these cards taped together like this?"

"It's a message from Ben," I said. "Do you know what it means? Death by hanging maybe? But that's not how he died." I remembered how that girl Zombie had talked about guys who liked to strangle themselves just for kicks. I shuddered.

"No. Death in tarot does not always mean death. It can mean ending. But the Hanged Man means *transformation*."

I was puzzled. Did it mean something like, "This transformation has come to an end"? Or maybe, "Death is not death, but transformation." "You sure know a lot for a dude who doesn't believe in any of it," I said.

"My job," he said, smiling. He'd been guzzling the fries all through his explanation. I realized I was getting restless. He must have noticed, because he suddenly said, "Time to close for lunch. You like video games?"

"Yeah . . . I happen to be the McDougal County champion at Bloodsucker, for one."

"Come with me. You are about to be learning one of the magic secrets of this bookstore."

He crooked his finger at me and beckoned.

CHAPTER 10

Through the Looking Glass

WONDERING, I FOLLOWED him, munching on the last few french fries out of the bag. I always like the ones at the bottom, because they're flat and crispy and they always seem to taste saltier.

The Far East Book Niche was kind of L-shaped, with the long side of the L fronting on the Boulevard. The short side was the occult section, with titles like *Mysteries of the Egyptians* and *Ancient Magic Practices You Can Emulate at Home*. The very back of the store was a bathroom. "Come along now," Guru Jack said. Openmouthed, I followed him into the cramped little toilet. He locked the door behind us. It was a grungy room, with mildew on the tiled walls. There was a full-length mirror on one wall.

Guru Jack turned off the light.

"Wait a minute—" I began suspiciously.

"Ah, you are not trusting me? You are thinking, I could be one of those crazy maniacs? Ha! But . . . perhaps you should be thinking of something else. How does a man like me, with a store like this in downtown L.A., make enough money to pay the rent? Well, there is this other L that nests inside the L that is the Far East Book Niche . . . and I am happening to be owner of both stores. Press your nose against the mirror, J.J. What do you see?"

I obeyed him. The glass steamed up a bit. But behind, I saw, as though through a fog . . . at first I thought it was the nightmare again, the tombstones rising out of the mist on the other side of the river. "No!" I said softly, and tried to back away. But then, looking closer, I saw that the tombstones had brilliant, flashing lights . . . and I heard a distant chorus of buzzes, beeps, and fragments of electronic melodies. "An arcade?" I said.

"Step through the magic mirror," Guru Jack said. "Into my palace of dreams. Where you can forget all your sorrows."

And then he like bowed, like a genie, and pushed what I thought was the toilet flush. Only it wasn't. It whisked the mirror to one side and I kind of stumbled into this tiny corridor that was only wide enough for one guy to kind of squeeze through. I could hear the arcade noises everywhere. There were three funhouse mirrors on the wall, and these video games were reflected, distorted, in them. That was why I had thought they were like grave markers at first.

Guru Jack reached into his robe and pulled out a handful of tokens. "What is your high score at Bloodsucker?"

"About ten million."

"Good. Not great."

"Fighting words, Guru Jack!" I said. Eagerly I elbowed my way toward the nearest Bloodsucker machine. It was crowded, and the jamming spot was already filled with other people's tokens. I decided to look for something else.

Finally I saw a game at the corner of the L that I'd never seen before. It was a western, shoot-'em-up kind of game—pretty bogus, but there was no one on it, so I decided to give it a try.

I was still wearing the headphones, so I turned them on full blast and let the pounding rhythm of the Vultures blast me into another dimension. The game was one of those laser disk ones that look ultrarealistic. There's one control for running around (you start off in the desert, but pretty soon you can mount a horse and go at double speed and you're hauling it through towns and chasing bank robbers and being ambushed by Indians and stuff like that) and there's another control for directional shooting. I was pretty much getting into it, even though I was used to seeing like more sci-fi or fantasy graphics. But a horse is just another kind of spaceship, so after a while I was totally jamming. I must have been on my first guy for like ten minutes. When I finally bought it, another guy popped in immediately.

But in the end there was no way out. I was hemmed in by a stalled stagecoach and I had fifteen whooping braves on my tail and this masked dude was leaping down on me from a butte. I was history.

When I died for the last time, the screen went dark and there was this awesome electronic sunset over this cemetery.

I saw it and started to think about death. And about how I shouldn't be enjoying myself. I should be thinking about why I had come here.

This is the kind of thing I was supposed to be thinking: I'd come on a grand, supernatural mission. Ben was the leader, the one with the great plan, and my job was to follow him. All the way to the journey's end. Ben always did the thinking for both of us. There was no reason for that to stop now.

I stood still for a moment, trying to recall some incident that would remind me of him and make me feel good about him. But instead I kept seeing other scenes.

Like the time he told that girl Cora Friedman my real name. Just because she kept asking him about it. She had thick red hair and a body that always seemed like it was going to burst loose out of her sweater and I know that was the only reason Ben told her. He would have told her anything.

He'd made her swear to secrecy but she couldn't help herself. It slipped out one day in school when she walked by me and I was trying to get my locker open. She just looked at me with vacant eyes and said, with total airheaded tactlessness, "Like, how's it going, Jeremiah Johnson?" I just stared at her because I couldn't believe that anyone had had the nerve to utter that name to my face.

I knew that Ben was in one of the science labs that period and I sprinted down the hall to find him. I didn't care about missing Mrs. Hulan's class. I wanted to punch him out or something. I stood at the door of the lab, shaking. Ben was the only one there, and he was heating something in a flash over a Bunsen burner. I screamed at him. "You told her! You told her!"

"What are you talking about? You're ruining my experiment."

He looked at me blankly. He didn't seem to care, didn't even seem to realize what that secret meant to me. I stood there, spluttering, and then I guess it dawned on him what I was mad about, and he just said, "J.J., you are so childish sometimes."

That was the memory that surfaced, and I was mad at Ben all over again, and mad at myself for remembering it. The brother I wanted to remember was totally perfect.

But as I was standing there getting madder and more confused, I heard my brother's voice again, faintly, through the barrage of bleeps and buzzes and the clink of quarters.

Ben's voice said, "It's nice to know, little brother, that you can reach the Forgetting Place even in a bustling arcade."

"Shut up!" I whispered. "You're not really here. I'm imagining you. Poof! Go away!" It occurred to me that I was still angry about him and Cora Friedman and my name. I started to feel guilty too now. I was supposed to be brooding about Ben, not losing my temper at him.

Then I saw his face in the video screen. He was barely visible. I looked around for Guru Jack, but the arcade seemed suddenly deserted. Oh, it was still full of people, but it was like reality had shifted somehow, like I was barricaded in a little pocket universe of my own and I couldn't reach beyond the invisible wall. Panicking, I shouted, "Get out of my life!"

"But you're so close to all the answers," Ben said. There was menace in his voice. I could hear him even though my CD player was going full blast.

"Maybe I don't want answers. Maybe I don't want to know."

"You've come a long way from the little brother who always wanted to imitate me, Jeremiah Johnson."

"What are you doing on the screen of a video game anyway?"

"All done with mirrors. You saw what the guru did in the bathroom? Same sort of thing."

I knew this was an illusion, that I was no more than half awake. I fiddled with the CD's controls but his voice still drowned out the music no matter how loud I made it. So I turned it off. The apparition was shadowy, and it shifted all the time so that I could only see it out of the corner of my eye. I was scared, I guess, but not that much, because this was like the visions I'd had on the bus coming west . . . a kind of totally intense daydreaming.

I watched his image in the glass. Suddenly I became aware of another face next to his. I couldn't tell if it was a girl or a boy. At first it seemed almost like that Japanese mask in the book, because the eyes looked so vacant. They could have been empty eyeholes. And the face was frozen, emotionless, as though it were carved from wood.

It took me a while to realize who was standing behind me. At last I said her name. "Zombie." She didn't move; for a moment I thought I'd made a mistake, that I was still stuck inside my waking dream. "What are you doing here? I thought I'd never see you again." I was relieved that it was someone I knew, even though we hadn't gotten along that well that day.

Light glimmered in Zombie McPherson's eyes.

Then . . . she seemed to see Ben's face. It seemed that the two images turned to one another and looked each other in the eye. Even though I knew Ben's was an illusion, it had to be something born out of my secret grief. . . .

"You *can* see him!" I said slowly.

Her lips parted, as though she were on the verge of saying something. I don't know if it was to me or to the shadowy image of my dead brother.

At first all I could feel was blind fury. "You don't have any right to see him," I said. "He's *my* brother. You don't know him, you never knew him."

And still she seemed to be gazing at Ben's face. For a moment the hardness was completely gone from her features. What was she, in love with a ghost, a shadow? Yet my brother's image seemed to become more and more real . . . or was it my own reflection? But we looked nothing alike. Or did we?

"If you can see him, then he must still be real, somewhere," I said. I clung to that shred of hope. "I'm not going crazy or anything."

Zombie's image looked into my brother's eyes. I saw something in those eyes—yearning? I remembered, suddenly, that she'd said, "I envy him." Emotions were flooding her. It was like the mask was fading out and showing the human underneath.

I turned, but she was darting away.

I tried to grab her arm. My hands grasped at the air. She dodged into a crowd of kids. All I could see was her Mohawk bobbing up and down.

"Zombie!" I shouted. All of a sudden it was like I had burst back out of that isolating force shield, and the noises and colors of the arcade were exploding around me all at once, battering my eyes and ears. I had to talk to her, had to find out if she had really seen Ben.

I followed. Someone shouted, "Hey, like I was here first!"

I was about to shove him, like I'd done with the TV newswoman. But some other dude held on to me. I watched helplessly as Zombie fled outside. For a second she was silhouetted in a rectangle of harsh light from outside. Then the door of the arcade slammed. A huge "No Loitering" sign swung back and forth.

I ran out onto the sidewalk.

The sun was brilliant. I shaded my eyes and tried to look for her. Was that her, running toward the corner of Comanche? I couldn't tell.

As I went back inside, I saw the name of Guru Jack's video arcade for the first time, in flashing letters over the doorway: Nirvana Games Unlimited.

I remembered that the Forgetting Place was Ben's private nickname for Nirvana.

Once inside I restarted the game (you could continue from where you left off if you put in a token within fifteen seconds, and I had only been a couple of seconds outside) but now I felt queasy about a game that had guns and shooting in it. So I just walked away.

I tried to get back into the Book Niche through the arcade's bathroom, but I couldn't figure it out. I had to walk outside again and go all the way around the block.

CHAPTER 11

The Mask of the Madwoman

"OH, THERE YOU are," Guru Jack said, looking up from the cash register. "I was hoping you would return. You like the arcade?"

"Huh? Oh, sure," I said, still distracted by my near encounter with Zombie McPherson. "It was great."

"I must go on an errand for an hour or so. You are not objecting to minding the store for me, isn't it?"

"Sure," I said. I guess I didn't sound too thrilled, because he reached across the counter and patted me on the head. I was surprised at being touched and started to shrink away. "Sorry," I said. "It's just—"

I wanted to tell him I was scared of getting close to people anymore. But I couldn't get the words out. I had a lot of pride. Too much, maybe. I think he understood, though. He didn't seem to take offense. Anyways he just said, "Tell you what, J.J. For the next hour, I am entrusting everything to you. If you feel like charging double, that is fine. If you feel like giving something away to the next customer who comes in, feel free. I am completely trusting your judgment."

"Give away?" I said, remembering how he'd just handed me that $29.95 book. "How do you expect to make any—" Then I nodded. "Oh. The arcade."

"I combine the spiritual and the commercial in a single enterprise," Guru Jack said in mystical tones. "The two halves of reality fit neatly together, isn't it? Yin and yang—good and evil—male and female—life and death—profit and loss—a video arcade and a transcendental bookstore."

"I don't know what you're talking about, but it sounds awesome."

"Totally awesome," he said in the same reverential voice.

"You're a Valley guru to the core," I said.

"Don't give away the store, though," he said. "Although, if I should be returning and finding the entire inventory gone, I shall merely be ascribing it to my karma. Or is it dharma?"

"You can never tell them apart," I finished for him. "Where are you going, anyways?"

"I am going to the mall to hang out," he said, and, tossing a loose flap of his robe over his shoulder, strode purposefully out the front door.

Nobody came in for a long time.

Beneath the cash register there was a stereo system that piped sitar music into the store. I hooked up my CD Walkman to it and soon the Vultures were blasting away. Then I refilled the incense burners, mixing up all the different kinds so that all the different fragrances were kind of mushed together and the smoke was swirling wildly over the reading area of the store. Still no one came in, so I wandered around taking books down from the shelves and shuffling them around. Obviously Guru Jack himself did this a lot, because most of the books weren't to be found in the categories they were supposed to be in. Under "Egyptian Magic," for instance, there was a cache of

sci-fi classics, Bradbury, Asimov, all that stuff. Also
some great titles like: *Evolution: a Communist Hoax*
and *Communism: a Diabolical Plot*. They were both
written by the same guy, a Swedish reverend. I
flipped through the pages of *Perpetual Motion: the
Latest Evidence* which had faded photographs of bizarre gadgets with blinking lights and cogs and
wheels and levers and spokes and computer key-
boards. Some of them made me laugh.

I tried hard not to think of what had happened in
the arcade. I didn't want there to be a link between
Zombie McPherson and my brother. And yet everyone
and every event that had happened since Ben's death
had seemed to connect with every other. "She didn't
really see him," I told myself. "Only me, my image in
the glass. That's the only possible explanation." Because it was embarrassing, and painful, the idea that
a stranger might be able to trespass on my most
private dreams.

"And yet," I thought, "if she really can see him, she
must be close to him in some way . . . and I ought to
get to know her better. Maybe she has another piece
of the puzzle."

I made my way to the other leg of the L, where there
was a section on tarot cards. I pulled out one book
and tried reading the definitions of "Death" and "The
Hanged Man." But they were confusing as hell, and
they gave ten or twenty different meanings for each
card, and most of them contradicted each other. But
still I couldn't help myself. I pulled out the double-
headed card and compared it with this book and that,
hoping to find some combination of meanings that
might make sense. Perhaps it meant, "Death is not
death, but transformation." But maybe it meant the
opposite: "Transformation is not transformation, but

death." If it meant the first, then Ben might be saying something like, "My body may be dead, but I'm still hanging around in some other form." But the other meaning was, "I thought things were going to change but instead I died." I didn't like that interpretation at all.

Another memory:

Late afternoon, the day of the Cora Friedman incident, we were kind of playing baseball in the backyard near the trees. Kind of because I was practicing and he was halfheartedly pitching to me while staring past me, through the trees, to the setting sun.

His pitches were totally lame and I was still mad at him. I guess he was trying to make up by condescending to play at all. But his mind wasn't in it. We went back and forth for a while and finally he just tossed the ball into the trees.

"No fair!" I said. "Do it again."

"Shut up."

"You spastic."

"I've got other things to think about."

"Like Cora Friedman. Betraying your own brother so you can get inside some girl's—"

"I'm sorry, all right? I'm sorry."

"Are you going to tell me I'm too young to understand about women, or something? Are you going to pull some kind of big-brother routine on me?"

"No." He seemed crushed. I didn't understand him at all at that moment. He was like a stranger.

He tried to hug me but I wouldn't give. I remember thinking, "He looks weak, he looks vulnerable." And not wanting to be like him after all.

But the Friedmans moved to the East Coast or

somewhere like that, and I'd never brought it up again. There weren't many times like that, I mean when he seemed like a stranger to me.

I closed the tarot card book. "That's one memory that belongs in the black hole," I thought, and tried to shove it back down into the Forgetting Place.

I must not have heard the bell in the front of the store. I jumped when I heard someone clearing his throat and rapping his knuckles on the counter.

"Excuse me. Do you have any books on Japanese drama?"

I went around to the front. There was a big cutout of some swami dude in the window display, but beyond I could see a familiar sight—the mile-long limo with the monster hood ornament. A bunch of kids had gathered around it. "Justin!" I cried out.

He was standing there, in a white uniform with silver trimmings, his cap under his arm. "Hey, let's have some service, man," he said. "I have to get back to the Valley in twenty minutes."

I came up to him. I was about level with the middle of his chest. "Japanese drama," I repeated dumbly. "You must be kidding."

"Hey, J.J.! Got a job selling loony fringe books, I see."

"It's only a temporary," I said. "Lots of room for advancement, though. Two hours ago I was a stock boy, now I'm the manager."

He laughed. "I didn't realize you were a disciple of the great Guru Jack."

"Are you?"

"Hell, no, I can't afford it. Tell you, he's a big shot in Beverly Hills. Goes to a lot of posh parties, you know? They say that hot new producer . . . what's his name

... Zottoli? ... won't do anything without consulting him."

"Not since his partner died," I said, remembering the séance I had seen.

"Holy—" He gaped. "You sure have picked up a lot of hot gossip in a few days, kid. I ought to tell Tygh about you."

"Get me a cameo in his video," I said, laughing.

"Can't, you're not in the union."

"Why do you need a book on Japanese drama?" There it was again ... another weird coincidence that seemed to lend weight to the theory that everything in the whole universe was linked to everything else ... fate, karma, "the force," whatever.

"Oh, it's Tygh who wants it. They're doing this samurai-on-an-alien-planet sequence and they wanted some pictures of Noh masks. It'll be at the concert they're giving next week. You coming?"

"Are you kidding?" I said. "Even weeks ago I heard it was totally sold out. We do get MTV, even in Kansas," I added in explanation. "We hear news about concerts."

"Might be able to do something." I guess my eyes must have bulged out of their sockets or something, because then he said, "After all, you do have contacts."

"Well, one, anyways."

"More than one," he said. I couldn't for the life of me figure out what he meant by that.

"I've got just the thing," I said, realizing now what I had to do. Maybe there was something to all this karma crap. I went to the back, got out the book, and handed it to him. "Don't worry about the $29.95. It's on the house."

"Hey, Tygh ain't a pauper, you know."

"You want me to give you a line about karma? Everything in the universe is linked to everything else—"

"I see the old man's really gotten to you."

I took the book and opened it to the page that had fascinated me so much earlier. . . .

"See this mask?" I said.

"Oh, yeah," he said. "It's beautiful." He stared at it for a long time. "It's almost alive. Yeah, it's just waiting for someone to breathe life into it. Yeah, yeah."

"You want a bag for it?"

"Sure. Let me pay for the bag at least. How about a buck?"

"I'll accept tips."

"How's life at the haunted house?"

"Could be worse."

He seemed to be waiting for me to say something else. I wanted to pump him for information about Zombie McPherson. But I didn't know how to begin. Finally I said, "So are you really the love of her life?"

"Oh, that! Just a running joke. I told you before, with her you gotta separate out the truth very carefully. With a strainer."

"Is she really a . . . hooker?"

"Sometimes," he said, looking down at the floor. "I think she does it to punish her father. She don't need the money."

"Her father . . ." The subject had finally been brought up. I hadn't wanted to pry, but the thing Zombie had said to me when we first met was bothering me. I mean, she'd kind of implied that her own father had . . . "Is it true?" I said at last. I couldn't hold in my curiosity anymore. "That her father . . . I mean, touched her."

"Her father's been dead for ten years," Justin said.

"She never forgave him for dying, I guess. Some things about him she remembers . . . some things about him she makes up."

"How can she stay angry for so long?" I said, wondering. "My brother . . . I mean, I couldn't be mad at him, I mean . . . it's not his fault he—"

Then, suddenly, all at once, this violent feeling seemed to erupt inside me. I didn't know what it was at first. It was just something that had been clenched up in me all this time and now it had to burst out. I *was* angry! That's what it was! My anger was an ugly thing. I was ashamed. I wanted to burst out crying but I didn't dare do it in front of Justin. I didn't even know who I was angry at, and then when I realized who it was, I started screaming hysterically. "Why did he die? How dare he die? What right did he have to kill himself?"

But Ben wasn't there to answer. And Justin just looked at me, uncomfortable. I realized I was shaking all over, almost torn apart.

Finally Justin reached out and touched me, very gently, on the shoulder. I guess I must have like flinched, because he snatched his hand away quickly and said, "Sorry, kid."

"I don't know," I said softly. "Hearing you talk about Zombie that way . . . I didn't know you could be angry at someone for dying." Was I still going to be that full of rage, ten years from now?

"But later, dude, I gotta go," he said, still uneasy.

"Wait—"

He paused at the door. "Yeah?"

"I, I, er, what's her real name, anyway? I bet her dad didn't name her Zombie, right?"

"Prudence," Justin said, shrugging. "Prudie for short."

As the door closed behind him, I remembered

something else Zombie had said: "I envy him . . . you try to see what's going to happen, sometimes you see it like so clearly, and you see there's no place to go anymore. At least he had the guts to get out on his own steam."

Did I envy him too? Was it better to die than to endure another argument about Perdue chickens? Did Ben know something I didn't? Well, maybe he did. I thought about my parents and Stephanie. About the new suit from Sears, neatly folded on my chair, the morning of the funeral. It occurred to me for the first time that Mom had gone out of her way to buy that suit because I'd refused to put on one of Ben's. It must have been an incredible pain to have to do that, with all the business of the funeral to take care of.

She did love me. I guess.

Had Mom and Dad been angry too? I wondered if they'd felt the same kind of rage as I'd just felt . . . I wondered if they'd been ashamed of that rage, like I had been. Was that why they'd never told me about it? If only they'd said something about it. If only *I* could have talked instead of shouting at them and punching out people.

But it was too late for regrets. I had blown the incident with the new suit and I had blown the funeral. And I wasn't in Kansas anymore. I was in Burbank and I had a mystery to solve.

Alone.

At last the guru came back. I wanted to tell him all about Zombie and about how Tygh Simpson's chauffeur had actually set foot in his shop, but he seemed distracted. I waved a hand in front of his face. "Sell anything?" he said.

"Well, I gave away a book."

"Do not be telling me. That book is never staying in my shop for longer than twenty-four hours." He pulled out a Styrofoam carton from his robe. "Lunch?"

"What is it?" I said. I opened it, but was just as mystified as before.

"Oh, caviar, *pâté de foie gras, canard à l'orange.*"

"What?"

"Leftovers from the shindig I am just returning from. They are entertaining very well around here, but I am the only one who has the nerve to be asking for a doggy bag."

"What kind of party was it?"

"I don't know. But there is always room for a token guru at any party around here."

"Did you know that Tygh Simpson's chauffeur was just in here?" I had to get the excitement out of my system.

"Oh, that's nice," said the guru, in a so-what kind of tone.

"I think they're going to use the mask of the madwoman in their concert," I said.

"Good," he said.

"Justin said he might be able to get me a ticket," I said.

He seemed interested at last. "Think he could wangle two?" he said.

CHAPTER 12

The Statue's Voice

WHEN I GOT back to Burbank that evening, Aunt Casey was talking on the kitchen phone. She motioned me to the refrigerator. I saw that she was busy, so I looked in the freezer for something I could microwave up in a hurry. I found a frozen dinner and popped it in.

She was saying, "Look, I can't be the one to tell him. It's up to you, you know."

Aunt Casey cupped her hand over the phone and said, "It's your parents. You will talk to them?"

"I have to, I guess," I said.

I took the phone. There was some static, and then I heard Stephanie bawling in the background. They were obviously in the kitchen, because I could hear the thrum of the dishwasher. The sound made me curiously homesick. Dad didn't get on the phone. Instead I heard him shouting to Mom, "You talk to him, honey. It's just too wrenching."

For the first time since it all started I think I felt sorry for Dad. I think I was about ready to come home that very moment, just knowing that he really was hurt.

112

"Dad—" I said. But I realized there was no one on the other end.

I could hear him calling for my mother again. But Mom didn't get on the phone either. Instead, it was Sissy Pavlat who picked up the phone. "Hi," she said.

"What are you doing there?" I was disturbed to hear her voice. She was an okay person, probably, but she didn't belong in my household.

"I've been staying over at your house," she said, "for the past couple of weeks. They're, like, upset, you know. You should have given them a chance. I mean, you were right in a way. They shouldn't have like gone to pieces. But you didn't exactly help. I mean, you were so unyielding. No one could touch you."

"What business is it of yours?" I said. "I want to talk to Mom."

There was silence. I heard someone crying somewhere. It wasn't like a kid crying for a toy. It was like this totally desperate weeping . . . the kind only adults know how to do. When they do it, there's no reasoning with them. It's like the whole universe has been destroyed. I was still wiped out from my outbreak of rage. I wanted to weep that way but I didn't know how to yet.

"Mom!" I shouted into the receiver. I wondered if she'd heard me. "Mom, stop crying."

Sissy came back. "See, you're making her cry," she said. "Come back, J.J."

I heard Mom screaming: "That bitch Casey told us she'd have him back right away! I hate all our relatives!" Suddenly I realized that they had known where I was the whole time, that Aunt Casey had probably been in contact with them all along.

I heard Dad's voice: "Dear, he has to have time to find himself."

He was back into that sixties psychobabble again. It made me sick. I said, "Sissy, tell them . . . I'm on the verge of this incredible discovery. I'm going to find out why it happened, I really am. After that we'll all feel much better, won't we?" I didn't believe it, but I wanted hard to, and I think Sissy did too. "I'll come home soon. I promise." Though I wasn't really thinking that far ahead.

"Wait," Sissy said. The sounds were cut off, so I knew that she had covered up the mouthpiece so that I couldn't hear something they were saying. There was a lot I wanted to say to them but I knew that if I started I would like explode or something. I needed them bad, but not the way I knew they were going to act. So I quietly replaced the receiver and went to my room.

The TV screen was blinking like crazy when I got there, and when I sat down at the keyboard to press Return, a new message appeared:

I GUESS BY NOW MOM AND DAD ARE START-
ING TO GET WEIRD, HUH, LITTLE BROTHER?
I BET YOU WANTED TO GO HOME WHEN YOU
FIRST HEARD THEIR VOICES. BUT THEN ONE
OF THEM PROBABLY SLIPPED OUT SOME FAT-
UOUS REMARK. SO YOU GOT MAD. IT'S ALL
RIGHT THOUGH. THEY'LL COME AROUND. IN
THE END.
    LOVE,
    YOUR BROTHER.

I resigned myself to the fact that he had been able to foresee every move I'd made so far. I couldn't believe in any kind of "ghost in the computer" theory. Staying in Aunt Casey's house, I'd seen plenty of evidence of how ghosts really operated.

I drifted into sleep watching the late late late late

late show. It was *White Zombie,* starring Bela Lugosi.
It wasn't gross like modern horror movies, but it was
plenty scary in its own way. I guess that's why I saw
Zombie McPherson in my dream. Oh, it was the same
old dream . . . the boat, the cemetery across the
water, the ferryman . . . only it was me with the
pole . . . the stench of dead leaves and human blood
in my nostrils . . . plying the pole against the squishy
mud at the bottom of the river. Yes. My own hands
were the hands of a skeleton. I was trapped in the
ferryman's body, but my mind was still my own, only
I couldn't speak because I had no tongue, no vocal
cords, only bone, dry, old, bleached, brittle. I looked
at the person who had come. It wasn't me. It wore the
mask of the madwoman. But from behind the mask, a
bright blue Mohawk protruded, so there was no
mistaking who it was.

"Where are you taking me?" she said. She sounded
drugged almost, or in a trance.

I wanted to answer, "I don't want to take you
anywhere," but I couldn't speak.

And Ben was standing on the opposite bank, sitting
on a headstone, his legs swinging back and forth. He
smiled at me. "We'll all be together soon," he said.
His voice was carried on the wind. The mist swirled.
His eyes glittered. I felt an intense longing to be with
him, even though I knew that I would never be able to
come back. "Death is not death, but transformation,"
he said.

I wanted to reason with Zombie. But I was met by
the empty eyes of the mask of the madwoman. There
was no emotion in the mask at all. At last I seized the
mask in both bony hands and tore it from her face . . .

And beneath the mask was another, and another,
and another.

*   *   *

The next morning was exciting. Guru Jack took me on a tour of Universal Studios.

It's pretty awesome. They have this tram that you ride in and you see a humongous King Kong and the shark from *Jaws* and they make rainstorms and snowstorms and they show you how special effects are done. I knew all about that already of course, because Ben was always able to recite all the technical details of things like that. I knew what a traveling matte was, but when they do it right in front of you, it's pretty thrilling. They put this kid from the audience on a bicycle and then made him look like the kid from *E.T.* We also saw the house from *Psycho*. The guide explained about how they used chocolate syrup instead of blood in that movie. I suddenly had a flash of the blood and the fallen leaves in the woods behind my house. I started to tremble, but Jack cracked jokes and I forgot about Ben for the rest of the morning.

Apart from the tour itself, they have these shows that they put on. Guru Jack and I laughed through the Conan show and the trained animal show, and then I went to this booth where they made me a *People* magazine cover with me on the cover for ten bucks. I thought it was kind of a rip-off but it seemed to make Jack happy. "You can be sending it to your parents, perhaps," he said. "They will be seeing that you are getting somewhere in Hollywood."

We even saw them filming an episode of *Still the Beaver*. Every kid in McDougal was going to be jealous of me, assuming I ever went home.

The afternoon was pretty routine, though. There was a woman whose husband had been gone for many years, but every couple of months or so she'd come down to Aunt Casey's for her fix. I hid in the statue and handled the controls with great skill, dimming the lights and making a shaft of eerie blue radiance burst across Aunt Casey's face as she shifted into the ferryman's voice.

Then there was a jock who wanted to ask his dead friend about some upcoming football game. It seemed he had a ton of money tied up in it.

Then there was some dude who wanted his dead wife to forgive him for finding a new girlfriend. Aunt Casey made the wife sound very understanding. I don't think she was really getting into it, though. That was more of a comforting and counseling kind of deal than any real psychic stuff. The man actually said, when he left, "She's grown so much more . . . compassionate, since she passed on."

Aunt Casey patted his hand consolingly. He went away smiling, since he didn't like have to feel guilty anymore.

The more I learned about it, the more I realized how much these people needed to feel that the dead were still around. They were willing to pay through the nose just for the illusion. I didn't exactly despise these people. But I started to take this whole spiritualism thing a whole lot less seriously.

Then, one day, the mile-long limo pulled up in front of Aunt Casey's house and deposited Zombie McPherson in the driveway.

She didn't see me because I was in the kitchen. But I saw Aunt Casey let her in. I wondered, "Where does she get that kind of money? A street kid shouldn't be able to afford Aunt Casey's rates." But I didn't want to think about it.

I saw her going into the séance room. Looking at the monitor, I saw that a few other clients were already sitting there. But they were just the usual bunch of the bored, the curious, the desperate.

Zombie went straight to the low table. She had

covered her face completely in whiteface, like a clown. Her eyes were circled in black, so that they seemed sunken, more like the sockets of a skull than like a human face. Her lips were painted white too, and she had sprayed white gunk on her Mohawk. She looked, well, like her name. And she still wore that long-sleeved jacket, even though she must be burning up under all that leather.

The group was making nervous small talk, waiting for the great medium to follow them in. Aunt Casey had come into the kitchen and was adjusting her hair and grabbing a quick bite of the pizza I had been fixing in the microwave.

"My psychiatrist always says this is so good for me," an elderly lady was saying. "He doesn't believe in it himself, but he's always saying how much more relaxed I am after I've talked to dear Uncle Rod. You know, a good cry is *so* therapeutic, isn't it?"

"Oh, yes," said her companion, another old woman wearing one of those hats piled with fruit and flowers that I thought they only wore in old movies. "My undertaker always says it helps me prepare for death . . . I don't know when it's going to come . . . it's my liver, you know."

I thought: "Zombie, you don't belong with those people . . . you shouldn't be thinking of death all the time . . . these people are practically dead themselves. That one already has her undertaker picked out, for God's sake!" But Zombie seemed to be joining in with the conversation.

I heard her say, "Me, like I'm trying to reach my father."

Of course! Her father, who she hadn't forgiven in all these years! I watched the monitor more attentively, glad for once that Guru Jack was back at the store; I wasn't in the mood for sage remarks about karma and dharma that I couldn't make head or tail of. I wondered how Aunt Casey was going to handle her . . . and whether she was going to make those accusations that she'd made to me, about her and her father.

"I know her, Aunt Casey," I said, pointing her out.

"Where do kids get that kind of money these days?" she said, sighing. "But I think I see she is not happy."

"She says she's happy, and strong, and she can't be hurt," I said. "And also . . . there's something with her and—" I was going to talk about the incident in the video arcade, but somehow it seemed so improbable that I thought she would laugh at me. So I let it drop.

"You care about her, do you not, J.J.? I sense it."

"Of course not!" I said. Too quickly. "I mean . . . well . . . I hardly know her. But she helped me. I still don't really know why."

"Well, since you seem to know something about her case, maybe you would rather not be in the statue today?"

"I can handle it." I said it more bravely than I felt.

Once I was snugly inside my control room, though, I let the by now familiar routine take over. Lights, camera, action! I felt totally powerful as I managed the slide controls and whipped up the wailing music to a terrifying intensity.

Aunt Casey slipped smoothly into her trance. The voice of the ferryman came, harsh and gravelly. I dimmed the house lights so that they were cloaked in darkness. I bathed Aunt Casey in this weird blue flickering light, so that her eyes seemed like the eyes of an alien.

"I see a figure . . . a figure draped in mist . . ." Familiar words. My cue to heighten the tension by turning up the music and by sending out the trusty old dry-ice fumes from secret vents beneath the bamboo matting.

"Oh, my God," one of them cried out. "It's Alicia, it's just got to be."

"Do not break the circle!" the ferryman's voice cried sharply.

I was really getting into the swing of things. I could see that Aunt Casey was totally jamming too. There was this big Oriental vase on a cabinet against the wall, and I flicked on the device that made it rattle. Someone screamed. It was the old lady with the fruit bowl hat. "Awesome! I wonder what her undertaker'll think of that!" I whispered. Sweat was pouring down her face. Aunt Casey spoke in a different voice now, the voice of another elderly lady. She had this snooty, New England kind of voice. "Ah, Millicent, my dear . . . how good to see you," she said. I could see the lump in Millicent's throat. Her eyes were totally popping out of her head. At first she seemed pretty comical, but the more I looked at her, the more I like felt what she was feeling. I could almost touch the inside of her mind, and what was in it wasn't this withered, prune-faced woman at all . . . it was more like a little girl, scared but full of joy too, because of hearing her dead friend's voice.

The more I was drawn into her feelings, the less I felt I was sitting at a console manipulating a bunch of special effects. Because her feelings were so real to me. They were—and it scared me to admit it to myself—they were the same feelings that I felt when I dreamed about Ben—or when I felt his presence and imagined him talking to me.

And the mist of dry ice swirled and became one with the mist of my dreams, the mist that shrouded the far shore of the river, the mist that cloaked the cemetery where my brother was waiting for me. . . .

The old woman and her companion were both weeping now. I turned to look at Zombie, who had been watching it all wide-eyed. At last, since Aunt Casey didn't say anything, and the old women were still sobbing, she spoke: "Dad . . . I want to talk to my Dad."

No one said anything.

Zombie said, "Are you there, Dad?" Her voice was tiny and frail . . . nothing like the arrogant way she'd spoken to me out in the streets of Hollywood.

There was no answer.

Then she said, her voice still like a very young girl's, "Daddy, why did you hurt me so much?"

Aunt Casey opened her eyes and it seemed like she was staring straight at me out of the monitor . . . hypnotizing me. I heard Zombie's voice again. It was a cry of total aloneness. It was what I felt when my brother was taken from me and no one seemed to know or care about what made him special to me.

Aunt Casey's eyes seemed to pierce right through me, like lasers.

I don't know what came over me. Maybe the real world and Aunt Casey's imaginary world were starting to blur into one another or something. Maybe I had been pulled into the same trance state she was in. But one moment I was in control and the next moment I was somewhere else completely. And my hands and fingers were moving on their own, flying along the console faster than a concert pianist. And then it was like someone grabbed hold of my mind and forced words from my lips, and they were broadcasting out of the statue's sound system . . . and it wasn't my own voice but a deeper, older voice. I had a whole 'nother image of myself . . . not a kid anymore but a grown man. I felt a powerful love for Zombie but I didn't think it came out of the mind of J.J.

Madigan. And I spoke to her: "Why do you seek me out, now, after all these years?"

"You hurt me!" Zombie cried. Like I wasn't ready for the total rage she was hurling at me. "You hurt me, Daddy!"

More words came from my lips: "You've been angry for so long. You hardly remember what I was really like. The person you're so angry with is dead and gone. What you've kept alive is a different person. You built a demon you could hate, but it's made of straw, you can tear it down . . . if only you dared . . . you have to free yourself, no one can do it for you."

As I heard myself speak, another part of me was thinking, "That's a terrible thing to tell her. Maybe it's true. But maybe it's not good to tear down her illusions like that."

"Forget me," the stranger's voice said. "Please, forget me." I saw that my hands were fiddling with the reverb control.

Zombie was shrieking at the top of her lungs, all the obscene words I'd ever heard in my life. It was contagious. The old women were screaming too, and Millicent was yanking her hand free, breaking the circle.

At that moment I snapped out of whatever it was. I turned the house lights way up. Zombie's face was garishly lit up and I saw tears streaking the dark circles she had drawn around her eyes, and the white makeup running down her cheeks and making white rivulets on her leather jacket.

I didn't know how I could face her. I didn't know who had put those words in my mouth. I was spooked, totally spooked. I slipped out of the back of the statue and sneaked into the hall.

At that moment, I heard this humongous roar. I thought, "Oh, God, an earthquake." I guess maybe I'd seen too many movies. Then I realized it was coming from out front. I opened the door.

This totally huge delivery truck was backing into the driveway. On the side was a picture of a gigantic candy bar and a freckled kid licking his lips. The truck kept backing up . . . and backing up . . . and up . . . and up . . . until the back of it was practically clobbering the front door.

I rushed forward. "Get out of here!" I screamed. "You're going to hit the house!"

The back of the truck swung open. With trucks like this you usually see heaps of crates or cardboard boxes. But there was nothing like that. Instead there were a couple dudes in heavy metal from head to foot, and they were lowering these steps down to the front porch. Then they started unrolling this carpet. Not a red carpet, but deep purple, spangled with stars and moons, all in gold stitching. I was so stunned that I didn't say anything when they laid the carpet all the way into the front hall.

Then, without a word, they vanished into the truck.

A figure emerged from the truck. He wasn't wearing any of those sci-fi clothes and he didn't have his face and hair done up in any bizarre way. In fact, he was kind of boringly dressed, in a T-shirt and blue jeans. He was a lot shorter than I thought he'd be too. But I didn't have any trouble recognizing Tygh Simpson, the lead singer of the Senseless Vultures.

"Did anyone see me?" he said to one of the heavy-metal dudes.

"No, boss. Coast is clear."

"Good move, taking the candy truck. The Valley *Times* had a field day when they found out about the hamburger truck . . ." He saw me and said, "Where's my sister?"

I was so stunned at having words addressed to me

by my absolute most favorite star that I just kind of turned into a statue.

He said, "Like, do you know where she is?"

"I—"

At that moment Zombie came charging out of the séance room. She took one look at Tygh and said, in a huff, "God, Tygh, do you have to follow me wherever I go? Why do you have to be such a total hoynt? Like, I can take care of myself, you know."

I looked from one to the other. "Sister—" I mumbled.

I kept staring.

Aunt Casey came in. "Oh, hello, Tygh," she said, "you are staying for dinner?"

"Why not?" he said. "I got a hour or so to kill before they haul me back to the studio." He whistled, and the heavy-metal dudes followed him inside. They were like bodyguards, I guess. "Sorry for the truck and all the other cloak-and-dagger business, but you know, like I can't travel around like a normal human being anymore . . . not since those groupies smashed the window of the old vulturemobile, crawled in, and tried to make off with my underwear."

"T-t-t-totally radical!" I said.

"Is he from Kansas?" Tygh said.

I didn't know whether to laugh or faint.

"Oh, and thanks for the book, J.J.," Tygh said.

He knew my name and everything! All of a sudden, I totally forgot that I'd about been ready to give up and go home only a few days before. I was so excited I could hardly breathe, and I was terrified that I'd get all hyper and stick my foot in my mouth.

"You're welcome," I said. I was probably bright red with embarrassment but I didn't care.

"What's for dinner?" Tygh said to Aunt Casey. "Antelopes' brains? Peacocks' livers?" He nudged me and said, "She's the world's greatest cook."

"Your favorite," Aunt Casey said.

"You didn't. No. Not human hearts in aspic."

I started laughing. "Not Human Hearts in Aspic" was always one of my favorite cuts on the Vultures' new album, and now I knew where it came from . . . it was a private joke between him and my aunt! I laughed so hard I almost didn't make it to the bathroom in time.

CHAPTER 13

Dinner With Vultures

MAYBE I WASN'T too talkative over dinner, but you can imagine why. But I still remember every single thing we had. Every course was from a different country. There was this frothy lemony Greek soup, then these awesome raw quails' eggs wrapped in seaweed and topped with fish eggs (I'm not kidding), then we had *filet américain*, which turned out to be raw hamburger. They are real big on raw things in Southern California, and even the cooked vegetables were kind of raw and crunchy. Considering what I'm used to, I think I did pretty well with all the weird food. Dessert was ice cream . . . or was it? It was sweet and sticky and gooey. Later I found out that it was lychee-flavored. Whatever that means.

We were eating in the séance room. With the lights at a decent level and all the sci-fi effects turned off, it was hard to believe everything that had happened only a couple of hours before. Guru Jack had turned up just as I was setting the table. He had an uncanny knack for sniffing out food. "My superior sensibilities," he told us. "We gurus are finely attuned to the oneness of the universe. Food here, hunger there . . . the attraction is part of the great cycle of being."

Then he lifted his little cup of Japanese sake and downed it in a single gulp.

Tygh laughed. "I can't believe how full of it he is," he said.

I said, "By the way, what *are* the lyrics in your songs? I mean, me and my friends, we're always arguing over what they say exactly. We can only catch a few words here and there . . ."

"Couldn't tell you," Tygh said.

"He's half out of his mind when he writes those songs," Zombie said resentfully. "Like, he's totally coked when he's composing."

"You know that's not true," Tygh said sharply.

"Go home!" Zombie shrieked at him. "You've got no right to come after me like this."

"I *am* responsible for you, you know."

"Yeah. Like you think you can be like Dad. But you're not. You're not that much older than me and you can't boss me around."

Tygh just shrugged. I got the impression that this was something he had to go through all the time. I couldn't see why Zombie couldn't leave him alone. At least in front of all these people. There was something going on between them—more than just your regular sibling rivalry. I realized how much she must feel lost and out of it, with her brother being so famous and all. Even I felt that way sometimes, because of how brilliant Ben was, and how much he knew about everything. I felt dumb all the time with him. But I reacted by trying to be as much like him as possible, while she was going for the opposite effect.

I saw something in Tygh's face that I had never seen in any of his music videos. It was a terrible kind of sadness. A loneliness, almost. I would never have known that a great star could feel that way. I mean, with all the money and all. And all that creativity.

"He always seems not to care about anything," I thought, "in those videos. He screams but there's laughter behind the screaming. He does violent things on the screen but you know it's casual, it's just a game." Yet there was a sorrow in his eyes that seemed to mirror my own sorrow. I said, softly, to him, "Tygh, I feel that way about my family too, sometimes. A lot." And I reached across the table and sort of patted him on the hand. I wasn't scared of him or anything anymore, because I knew he was human.

"You're a great kid," he said, and patted my hand back. "Friends for life?"

"Totally."

"Jesus!" Zombie said. "Like, what a couple of fags! You've only known him for an hour and you're already his best friend. Well, for your information, if I can like break up this full-on convo for like just *one* second—"

"I'm listening," everyone said at once.

Zombie got up from the table. Since we were all sitting on floor cushions, we had to stare upward to see her face, and she kind of towered over us, brandishing a chopstick, like a pissed-off Statue of Liberty.

"I spoke to Dad today." She was looking Tygh in the eye when she said this. "You never did that. I heard his voice. It was so real—"

"You don't even remember his voice," Tygh said.

"I heard it! I knew it! You didn't hear it, so shut up!"

In the pause I studied the faces of the others. "The girl's crazy," I thought. But what had possessed me, what had wrung those words out of me? If Zombie was really going mad or something, was I responsible for sending her over the edge? It was a scary thought, and I felt cold inside.

"I found out something," Zombie said. "I found that he's really dead. Really."

"You already knew that," Tygh said gently.

"Maybe I did. But I never believed it. You know what else he said? He said I have to free myself, that no one can do it for me. So leave me alone, big brother, let me handle my own life from here on out. I'm going to do what I've always meant to do. Nothing's going to stop me. I have to free myself. Yeah, totally."

But was that really what it meant? I was incredibly uncomfortable, sitting there, knowing what she'd heard had come out of me, somehow, knowing that she took every word of it as gospel truth, a genuine visitation of the supernatural. I could see that even Tygh, who must have been used to Zombie's moods, was surprised by her this evening.

"You're getting hysterical," Tygh said.

"I'm getting out of here," Zombie said. And she made a grand exit, kind of like she'd been accepting an Oscar or something. There wasn't any applause, though. Everyone kind of sat, fidgeting, as we heard the front door slam and Zombie's voice calling for Justin.

"I don't know what to do about her," Tygh said at last. "I've sent her to the most expensive analyst in Beverly Hills. She can have anything she wants. Like, I mean, she's my only sister and I love her." He sounded real apologetic, like I wasn't going to believe him or something.

"I do believe you," I said. "But I think it's your time she wants, not gifts."

"Maybe. But when I do spend time, it always ends up like this."

"I don't know, Tygh. Anyways, who am I to give family counseling to my greatest idol? I can't even deal with my own family."

He laughed sadly.

"Well," the guru said, "I for one am wanting some coffee." He went into the kitchen. I heard him grumbling, and then I heard something metal crashing to the floor.

"I'd better see what he's up to," Aunt Casey said. And followed him out.

Suddenly I found myself alone with Tygh Simpson, lead singer of the Senseless Vultures . . . talking to him like he was my best friend or something. What a trip.

We didn't say anything to each other for a long while.

At last, I said, "Your dad . . . I mean, that supernatural experience she had . . . I don't know what to say, I mean, I think I had something to do with it."

"She really likes you."

"What? But she never has anything good to say to me."

"She talks about you a lot. She says you understand her a lot better than I do. Maybe she's right."

"But you're her brother! You must know her better than anyone else." Then I thought to myself, "But I thought I knew Ben better than anyone else . . . and look how wrong I was."

He said, "Sometimes it takes someone from outside to see something that's been staring you in the face for years and years and years."

I thought of Ben and his weird ideas about predicting the future and psychic powers and I wondered if maybe he was just mixed up, plain crazy, not this mega-brilliant visionary genius I'd always seen him as.

"I don't think I understand her at all. But I've been as angry as she has, I think."

"She really likes you." Tygh smiled wryly. "She thinks the world of you. Sometime, when she's not feeling so hysterical, you should ask her out, J.J. I'd like that."

"Are you playing some kind of trick on me?"

"I can daydream about matching my sister up with a nice, good-looking, all-American boy from Kansas, can't I? Hold it, pick your jaw off the table, little brother!"

God, it really hurt when he called me "little brother." And I knew he didn't mean anything by it. I mean, he wasn't trying to take Ben's place or anything like that, but it still hurt anyways. And right away he saw that and he became uneasy. And I didn't want him to feel that he'd hurt me, because I really liked him. A lot. And not just because he was the great Tygh Simpson either.

So I pestered him about the lyrics to his songs again.

"Tell you something," he said. "Once, when we were on tour in Japan—"

"I saw it on MTV!" I said excitedly.

"—we went to see this ancient Japanese drama. They're called Noh plays. There was this one story we saw . . . about a madwoman in search of her lost child?"

"*Sumidagawa.*"

"You must be psychic."

"Guess so."

"Anyway, none of us understood a word of it. Like, it was all in Japanese, you know? But hell, it really *communicated.* The weird stylized gestures, the wailing of the flutes . . . but you know, I found out that most of the people in the audience didn't understand much of it either . . . these plays are all in this twelfth-century language, you see. Now and then there'd be a word floating out of the mess of incomprehensible words, and you could grasp the word for a moment and think you knew what they were saying . . . but then it would vanish and you'd be adrift. It was like that even if you spoke the language, which we didn't. I thought that was a totally brilliant concept. So I started to do my songs that way. Because life's like that. We're all lost in the mist, floating down a one-way river, and now and then we see something, but then it's gone. We see weird buildings sometimes, or faces we almost recognize but not quite, or—"

"Gravestones," I said quietly, because he had brought my dream to the surface of my mind. I was frightened, but full of a strange joy too, because I felt that he had been to the place I had seen in the dream.

"Yeah. Gravestones. I've been there. Zombie doesn't remember Dad at all, but I do. I was your age, but she was only a toddler."

"I'm not alone," I thought, wonderingly, to myself. "Where's your mom?" I said. After I said that I wondered if it was okay to ask, or whether I was dredging up some long-forgotten pain.

He said, "She blew after Dad died. I haven't seen her since. My agent took care of us, though. You know I was doing some session musician work even when I was quite a young kid. The cute choirboy's voice in the old Toasted Apple Crunchies commercial, that was me. You don't remember it, I'm sure."

"Guess not." I had to smile at the idea of Tygh Simpson the cute choirboy. "What a concept."

"I bet your brother was a pretty cool dude."

"Yeah." Tygh *did* understand how I felt about Ben! I was furious with myself for doubting Ben a moment before and thinking he might have been mixed-up and crazy.

"Why did you run away from home?"

"To find the Forgetting Place."

"The Forgetting Place." He seemed to be turning that phrase over in his mind. "That would make a great ballad."

"You're welcome to it," I said. For the first time, I felt a little bit able to share my brother with someone. And I wanted to share him so much. I wanted to trust Tygh with Ben's secret name for Nirvana. It made me feel less alone somehow.

"Tell you what. I hear you couldn't get a ticket for my concert Friday. Here—" he reached into his jeans. "A bunch of backstage passes."

"Oh—my—God."

"I meant what I said. Give Zombie a call, okay? I promise, she's not always that way. She can be a sweet girl. Really. I know it's hard to believe."

I just stared at the pieces of paper he had thrust into my hand. Everything started to vibrate and I thought it must be another L.A. earth tremor, but it turned out to be me, trembling.

"Later, kid."

He got up and left the room, leaving me still quaking with excitement and anticipation. I looked up and saw Aunt Casey and Guru Jack looking at me oddly.

"Well, don't keep us in suspense," Jack said. "How much will you be wanting for one of those tickets? Or is my karma such that I may be able to be wangling a small gift from my faithful disciple?"

"Of course!" I said, dancing up and down on the

straw. "You can have as many as you want!" I threw the backstage passes in the air and let them rain down on me.

This was awesome. I was really happy for the first time since all this had begun. I was so hyper I didn't get to sleep until after five in the morning, long after the late-night double feature had given way to snow and hissing.

CHAPTER 14

The Man From the Webb Foundation

SOMEHOW I SUSPECTED it was because I had been so exhilarated that evening. Anyways, the bad dreams were even worse, even more vivid, that night.

I'd only slept for two or three hours when I couldn't stand it anymore and woke up. It was midmorning. There was a message on the monitor: BY NOW I BET YOU'RE STARTING TO REALLY GET INTO IT, LITTLE BROTHER, AREN'T YOU? YOU'VE PROBABLY BEEN SUCKED INTO ONE OF THOSE TRANCES OF AUNT CASEY'S. MAYBE YOU'VE EVEN BEEN POSSESSED BY ONE OF THE DEAD. THAT'S OKAY. I BET YOU'RE A WHOLE LOT LESS SKEPTICAL ABOUT THESE THINGS THAN YOU WERE WHEN YOU STARTED, RIGHT?

I think I screamed. I wanted to get up and pull the plug on Ben. But then I felt terrible feelings of disloyalty. So I didn't move. Anyways, I was too tired to drag myself out of bed.

I must have screamed, because, just as I was drifting off again, Aunt Casey came in to see me.

"You want to eat?" she said. She had brought this lacquer tray that was literally piled with goodies . . . everything from French toast to poached salmon.

"Food cannot solve every problem, but at least you feel better while you are brooding about it."

"I'm upset, damn it!" I said weakly. But then I rubbed my eyes and saw her standing there, her face full of concern, and I said, "I'm sorry."

She sat down on the mattress and started to cut up the French toast with a fork. "I can feed myself," I protested.

"Sometimes good for you to feel like a baby," she said. "Something that girl needs to learn."

"Yeah, really." We smiled at each other. "You're so good at—like, caring for me, I guess." I took a healthy bite of the French toast. "What happened yesterday really scared me pretty good."

"I can imagine."

"Do you think I was really possessed by the spirit of . . . her dad? I mean, an ordinary kid like me, not *into* any of this stuff like my brother was?"

"Could be. What do you think? Finish chewing before you answer."

I thought about it awhile as I swallowed my food. "Well, maybe I was under the control of some ghost. But maybe not. I mean, like, everything I said was something I knew already. Because Tygh's chauffeur was in the store and he told me a lot of stuff."

"That is secret of most miracles, J.J.," she said, thoughtfully stroking my forehead. "They are not miracles to the people who perform them, but the performer is not person that counts, is it? Ask Tygh about it sometime. Music is magic too. And it too uses misdirection, and sleight of hand, and knowing things the audience doesn't know you know. But that does not make it any less magical or less musical."

"That doesn't sound right," I said. "I mean, things shouldn't be that way. It makes it all sound so . . . I don't know, mechanical. Soulless. Cheap."

"Can it be soulless when you touch a person so profoundly? No, J.J. Art is deception. We tell lies that add up to great truths."

When she put it that way, I realized how much power there was in what we did. We could change people's lives. No, there was nothing cheap about that. But that made it even more frightening. It had seemed like a game at first, a kind of make-believe that rich dudes were willing to shell out big bucks for. Now it was still make-believe but it was true too. "How can something be true and false at the same time?" I said, trying to make light of it.

"That's the real difference between a kid and a grown-up, isn't it? Kids really believe things, and, well, maybe adults do not."

I was totally afraid when she said that. Because she echoed something that I had come to fear more and more in the past couple of weeks. I was going to be an adult one day. Because I was losing my sense of things being absolute: good and evil, truth and falsehood. She was telling me that this was one of the symptoms of being an adult.

Well, that was fine and dandy, and growing up was pretty important, I guess, but . . . I just didn't like many adults. I mean, my parents? I loved them, of course. But in their case, being grown up didn't seem to mean they were any better off than me, except that they had credit cards. I knew where I stood in the world. At least, I knew up until Ben died.

I liked Aunt Casey and the guru, of course. But maybe it was because they both seemed to be able to switch back and forth from the grown-up world to my world. "If I grow up . . . if and when," I said very earnestly, "I want to be like you and Jack, not like my parents. I don't want to have something inside me *die*, just in order for me to be able to own a car and a home and have kids of my own."

She said, "I see. You do not want Death; you want the Hanged Man."

"You understand!" I said, grinning suddenly. Maybe there was something to this kung fu "Grasshopper" routine.

"Your parents have their good points. You didn't know them back in the sixties."

"Oh, the sixties, the commune, all that junk. I've been through the photo albums again and again. You're right, I can't even imagine them like that. How did they become the way they are now, how did they become so empty?"

She looked at me very seriously and said, "You think they are empty?"

"Well, but they're so . . ." I thought of all those sixties buzzwords they were always spouting. "I mean, the way they talk and all . . . they think they're living in a rerun of *The Partridge Family* when really it's . . . life's not like that."

"So wise," she said. I wasn't sure if she was making fun of me. "What *is* life like?"

"I don't know."

"But you think they ought to know."

"Well, of course! They're grown-ups. But they act like kids sometimes. Worse than kids."

"Is that so wrong?" Aunt Casey said.

I'd never thought about that. I mean, kids are supposed to act like kids and adults are supposed to act like adults. For the first time I wondered how *I* was "supposed" to act. After all, I was neither.

"Think about it. You have to know the answer. Best, before you see them again."

"Before I see them again . . ."

"You are going to see them again, you know. And I want to tell you something about your parents. When

I married your Uncle Elbert, a lot of people were shocked. They didn't have all that many mixed marriages in those days. Maybe your parents were shocked. But of all Elbert's relatives, they were the only ones who tried the hardest to accept me. You can put it down to sixties buzzwords if you want, but they really tried to live by those buzzwords, you know."

It was hard to imagine my babbling parents as idealists. But I found myself thinking, "If I go back, I'll try to see behind the way they are now . . . to the way they used to be."

But they seemed so far away. I knew I would have to go back, eventually, that I couldn't just stay here forever. But my parents seemed so remote, and this strange place, so full of deception and illusion, so, so real . . . as far as I could see, my parents were across the river too, among the gravestones with my dead brother.

This guy came to see me that afternoon and insisted on talking to me alone. I thought it was the FBI at first—maybe my parents had sicked them on me when they discovered I wasn't coming home. This dude had a Secret Service sort of aura about him: dark suit, dark glasses, dark tie, dark hair, totally pale, bloodless-looking face. I was expecting him to pull out his badge and throw me against the wall and like strip-search me or something.

It was even worse than that, though. He was from the Webb Foundation.

I told him to get out.

"Now wait a minute," he said. He had a very gentle voice, actually. I'd expected him to take a totally Rambo-like tone, you know, blow me away with an M-16 if I didn't heel. "I'm very interested in you, and I'm really sorry about your brother, B.B. He was a fascinating individual. Very brilliant, I think. Couldn't we just talk?"

"Oh." We were in the hall. Aunt Casey was busy in the séance room. I didn't quite know where to take him, so I led him outside and around to the back, where there were a couple of deck chairs by the pool. I had my CD headphones on, although nothing was playing. I just wanted to give him the impression that the interview would soon be over. Because, even though he was acting kind, he made me nervous.

"Whatcha listening to?" he said.

"Vultures," I said, hoping to confuse him. Most people over thirty don't know who the Vultures are. And this guy was really old—maybe thirty-five.

"Oh, radical," he said. (Since people didn't say that anymore around here, as I had been told again and again and again, I realized that he must desperately be trying to sound hip so that I'd think he was one of the guys.)

"You don't have to try to talk like a kid," I said—I wasn't being nasty, I just wanted to level with him—"I can speak English, too."

He seemed nonplussed for a moment, then he said, "Oh, ha, ha, very funny."

"You're not planning to recruit me for your foundation, are you?" I said. "Because if you are, the answer's no. For all I know, maybe you're responsible for Ben killing himself."

"Oh . . . not at all . . . but we'd love it if you would come down for some tests. You know, psychic talents often run in families. And your brother was *really* sensitive to, well, time lines, you might call them."

"You're saying he could predict the future."

"Sort of. There's never just *one* future, you know . . . just a series of infinitely converging possibilities.

Mind if I give you a few simple tests?"

"Oh, no, you don't."

He looked kind of disappointed. Anyways, the sun was out, glaringly bright. The sky was clear and the water glittery. It just didn't seem like the right atmosphere for something horrifying to happen. So after he looked at me with this "aw, c'mon, shucks" expression for a while, I said, "If that's all it is. But I warn you, I'm no good at those cards."

He pulled out a stack of them from his coat pocket —I thought he must be sweating like a pig under all that dark clothing—and started shuffling them.

I said, "Now, let's get it right. They're stars, circles, wavy lines, stuff like that?"

"Oh, you know about it."

"The first one's the wavy lines."

He looked kind of surprised, then turned the card over. It slipped onto the tiles faceup. "What do you know?"

I got the next couple wrong, but then I got four or five in a row. "Hey, I'm jamming at this," I said.

"Yeah. You want to participate in our big new 'predicting' network?"

"No," I said firmly. "Not in a million years. You're not recruiting me. For all I know, what my brother saw killed him."

"He killed himself, J.J."

That was brutal of him but I guess it was true. I got the next ten cards wrong. A lot of this depends on your mood, probably. Several times I caught a flash in my mind of that it was, but I deliberately gave a different answer.

"Think of us, okay?" He got up to leave.

"That's it?"

"Yes," he said.

"Doesn't run in families after all?"

He nodded. I felt an incredible sense of relief. Maybe that business in the séance had just been an isolated incident. I was more interested in Tygh Simpson's upcoming concert than I was in weird powers. A horror movie's a horror movie and life is life.

I showed him out. I watched him through a crack in the door as he stopped to admire the rock garden. He stooped to snoop behind the biggest rock (maybe Aunt Casey habitually left messages there) and then walked to this gleaming silver Porsche that was parked at the curb. "I guess there's a lot of money in all this nonsense," I said to myself.

"Certainly," came my aunt's voice. I jumped. "Sorry to startle you."

"I was saying, he must make a lot of money going around testing people."

"Psychic research," Aunt Casey said, "grant city. Rich people leave them huge bequests. Want to make sure someone's still trying to stay in touch with them, after, you know."

"You think that's what Ben is doing?" I said bitterly. "Making sure he's not forgotten?"

I got Tygh's unlisted number from Aunt Casey and tried to call Zombie. I didn't see what good it would do, but it's not every day a big star tries to fix you up with his sister.

I got a secretary or someone. She knew who I was, which surprised me. She told me that no one was home, but that she'd make sure they knew I called.

Guru Jack turned up, so I decided to ride with him to the store. I just didn't feel like hanging around, and I had a nagging fear that the man from the Webb Foundation might be prowling around among the azaleas. Or hiding in the little hut by the pool.

If I got bored of the store, I could always slip through the mirror with a handful of video tokens. Like, maybe Bloodsucker wouldn't be so crowded, and I'd be able to rack up a few million points before becoming history.

CHAPTER 15

Bloodsucker

THE NINJA DUDE, who had been working the morning shift, nodded at us, left the register, and shuffled off outside. Even though everything on the Boulevard was so garish as to make your eyes smart, he still managed to blend in, totally inconspicuous in his medieval Japanese assassin's costume. No one even glanced at him twice. I remarked on it.

"That is being a splendid example of anonymity a big city can be providing," Guru Jack said smugly. "After all, here I am in my saffron robes, and nobody is noticing me either. It is a wonderful side benefit of having a bookshop in Hollywood. I mean, if you could imagine for a moment what it would be like if some heavy-metal personage walked down the street in downtown Delhi? Even the sacred cows would stop to stare."

The Lex Nakashima edition of the Japanese Noh plays was lying on the counter. There was a note from Tygh: "Hi, Jack, get it, ha, ha? Seriously, I couldn't keep this $29.95 book without paying. All I needed was the pictures, so I Xeroxed them. Please pass the book on to some other deserving person."

"Jack!" I said, all excited about the coincidence.

144

"The book—it's back again!"

Guru Jack shrugged. "I know."

Not for the first time since running away from home, I felt I was witnessing a running gag and I wasn't being let in on the joke. Or was it karma? Ordinary people would talk about uncanny coincidences, but . . . I just gave up and took the book to reshelve it. I was thinking about trying to call Zombie again, but instead I decided to go through to the video arcade.

This time it was pretty empty. I must have hit the dead spot right after lunch, when a lot of people are just too bloated to stagger down for their video game fix.

The dude who was working the change booth recognized me as a crony of the guru's—talk about friends in high places!—and immediately handed me a pile of tokens, and when I tried to give him a dollar he just said, imitating Jack's accent, something like "cycle of being awareness awesome karma."

There were a couple of kids furiously working a beat-up old Galaga game, but, to my delight, there was no one on Bloodsucker. I made a beeline for that game. After all, I am the McDougal County champion, and I even made it into the local paper on that account once, when I played for four hours on the same quarter.

Actually, though, I have always suspected that Mr. Woodley, who owns the place, kind of tampered with the hardware so that he could like get the extra publicity for that retarded arcade of his.

I suspected that even more when I was disgustingly defeated in the first ten seconds of the game. It's a pretty awesome game as regards graphics. The best part about it is that you get to be the bad guy—the monster—the Count, whatever. And you are fleeing like crazy down these corridors and passageways with these totally cool scenes that look like the cover of *Fangoria*, you know, headless dudes and zombies with exploding brains, all that neat stuff. You're being chased by this dude who's about to hammer a stake into your heart . . . and when he gets you, the graphics are about as close to R-rated violence as you can get. Blood spurting everywhere. It's the kind of game that would have made my brother throw up.

On the third token, my reflexes started to take over and I made it through the third crypt, which is where some of the walls have spikes and start to close in on you. That's when I bought it—one of the spikes happened to get me in the heart, which was just bad luck because they almost always miss and you have to run into them just so for them to get you.

I was crushed to death like something in a garbage compactor. Blood was exploding on the screen like fireworks, and there was this totally realistic ripping sound, like human flesh being torn apart. At that moment—

I seemed to be caught inside another instant of time altogether. The blood was still cascading all around me. But I heard a pistol go off somewhere, far away . . . felt the dry leaves falling from the sky . . . touching my face . . . leaves flecked with human blood . . . and I heard my own voice, far, far away too, crying out . . . and I knew it was an image out of the dark place in my memory . . . an image I thought I'd lost forever.

Had I actually seen him do it?

I was shaking. The screen was flashing like crazy. It was telling me that I'd made high score.

The vision slipped away, and I tried to grasp it again . . . I was afraid to catch hold of it because I knew it was something infinitely terrifying . . . but I knew I had to bring it back up to the surface . . . I reached out with my mind . . . I saw the dark place retreating and retreating and retreating like the door in a dream of a corridor you can never reach the end of . . . like the other shore of the river . . . and then, for a fleeting second, I saw another picture, vivid, against the bloodred of the video screen . . . Ben's face. Half of it anyway. The other half . . . I guess it was torn away. And he was trying to speak to me, to move his lips, but already they were clogged with blood.

Then it was gone and there was someone else's reflected in the monitor. "Zombie," I said. Her face, against the crimson background, seemed somehow softer, warmer than it had been before. Slowly I turned around.

Yeah, it was her all right. But she had changed somehow. It wasn't really in her way of dress. She still wore the leather jacket that I'd never seen her without, but she was carrying a lot less in the way of heavy metal. It was her face that was different. She'd unglued her Mohawk so that it kind of spidered over the rest of her scalp. And she had painted the top of her head with these geometric designs, all in pale blue. She wore no regular makeup at all, and for the first time I saw how young she looked. I'd always thought of her as being older than me—because of her street smarts, maybe, or because of her constant tough talk and foul language—but now she seemed kind of my age or maybe even younger.

"Don't stare, it's rude," she said. But she smiled and I knew she didn't mean it as a put-down.

"It's well, actually, I wasn't staring—"

"It's like a Jekyll and Hyde deal, isn't it?" she said.

"My thoughts exactly."

She looked at my score. "Only 159,672?" she said scornfully.

"I used to turn it over all the time in McDougal."

"McDougal?"

"My hometown."

"Well, like this is the big leagues now here. Bet you I can beat you."

"Come on, that wouldn't be fair. Besides, girls always suck at video games. They don't have the motor reflexes."

"Chauvinist!" She rolled her eyes.

"Anyways, how did you know I was here?"

"Got your message. Want to make something of it?"

"Let's just play."

"What are the stakes?"

"I don't know. Your mansion against my CD player." Which, for once, I had left back at the house, along with all the other stuff in the Jiffy Bag, because I couldn't cope with it all at the moment.

"The mansion's held by a trust or something," she said. "Besides, Tygh owns everything, I just live there. Somewhere in the back of the house with my own separate entrance so no one will see me and I won't embarrass anybody."

"Okay. Well then, if I win—as I definitely will—you have to be nice for a whole hour. No nasty remarks. No dramatic accusations. Just, you know, normal."

"I am being normal right now, stupid."

"Relatively." I gave her a token and prepared to see her make a fool of herself. After all, even though I hadn't been playing too well just now, I *was* the county champion, wasn't I? And competition would really get me going. We dropped our tokens and pushed the two-player button.

"After you," I said.

"After you."

"After you."

"Oh, all right, after me." She started playing. Most people play with a lot of like violent body language, but Zombie's arcade style was just what her name might suggest. She stood there, staring glassy-eyed at the screen, and her hands moved like lightning, completely independent of one another. There's this one location in the first maze where you can duck in and hide. It's a shabby old treasure chest with its lid half open. Most people zoom right past it, but she knew the path where you jump down, wait for two beats, and allow the dude with the stake to run right on by.

I must have registered surprise, because she said, "Didn't think I knew that one, did you?" I was even more astonished, because I can't really carry on a conversation when I'm totally jamming in Blood-sucker because it ruins my concentration. But her hands went on, moving as though they had brains of their own. She said, "I was going to be a concert pianist once. This is from all the exercises I used to do. I'm on autopilot now. I'm not even thinking about the game. You know when I'm on the street some-times and I let some dude pick me up, I'm on autopilot then as well, like my mind is in a whole 'nother country, and like I'm thinking about someone completely different than the one I'm with."

"Who are you thinking about now?"

"You, I guess." That really threw me. I felt my cheeks flush a little.

Her, too, because she lost her guy in a spider's web that came swooping down from the ceiling. On this level, all you have to do is jump up and down to break the web. It's only after the seventh or eighth screen that you have to claw, bite, or slice your way out. "Stupid of me," she said.

I played for a while, but my heart wasn't in it. It's hard to be concerned about a video game when you're being flooded by all these confusing feelings and when you're with a girl who's giving you all these contradictory signals. I mean, what were the rules around here, anyways? I couldn't very well ask her to the Friday night dance in the gym. Finally I succumbed to the same mistake she had and I watched my vampire being devoured by a giant spider. I kind of felt that way myself. It wasn't an unpleasant feeling, though.

Then I watched Zombie climb up to the tenth screen without even turning a hair. She wasn't even sweating under that leather jacket. The arcade was starting to get more crowded; one or two people were hunched behind us, watching curiously.

She said, "Did I startle you last time? I mean, coming up behind you and all. In the arcade. The other day. In case you've forgotten."

"Yeah, I was really shocked. You see, I thought . . . I thought you were looking at someone else . . . reflected in the glass."

"That's odd. I did have some kind of weird sensation that I was, like, peering into some other world. And I did see someone. But then I saw he was really you. Die, die, die!" It took me a moment to realize that she was saying that to the video game. "Why can't you die forever?" It was the first time she'd appeared to show the slightest interest in the game, and it was around the fifteenth screen and still her second guy.

"But who did you think it was at first?" I said.

"What do you care?"

"It's just that—"

"My father," Zombie said softly. "That's who I thought I saw. Maybe that's why I bolted. I always used to imagine these long, long conversations with him. But now I don't anymore. Ever since . . . something that happened during the séance. Did you hear about it?"

I was stuck for an answer. What was I supposed to say, that the voice had been my voice, that I had somehow pried dark secrets from her mind and used them on her? "So it wasn't my brother at all," I said.

"Of course not. I don't even know him. Knew him, I mean."

"But you told me you envied him—"

"Sure. But just because of that doesn't mean his ghost is going to start appearing to me."

Suddenly this thought occurred to me. Ben didn't know Zombie McPherson . . . had never met her . . . Zombie McPherson was the first person in my life whom my brother didn't know . . . that this relationship was the first thing in my life that was not at all a part of him. It's like I was bound to my brother's memory with a rope, and one of the strands was fraying. I was dismayed at it, but I felt a kind of pride too. Maybe I wasn't going to be a reflection of him forever.

I didn't have to share Zombie with anyone. I was starting to understand how Ben felt about that Cora Friedman girl. How this special feeling he had could have pushed him all the way into betraying me, his one and only best beloved and loyal brother.

Well, maybe I was a little bit less loyal now.

And I wasn't even feeling that guilty about it. That was the weirdest thing.

Someone behind us yelled, "You dudes are more fun than the game. Have you ever thought of trying out for a soap opera or something?" Suddenly I saw that the crowd had really gathered around the Blood-sucker machine, and that they'd all been listening to every word we'd said to each other. Zombie and I looked at each other, laughed, and then I said, "Maybe we ought to blow."

"Yeah." She turned to the kid behind us, a tiny, skinny thing with new wave sunglasses. "You can play the rest of this guy."

"Rad!" he said in a piping little voice.

Zombie grabbed my arm. It was the first time she had ever touched me. Her hand was cold and dry. She led me out of the arcade. "Where are we going?" I said.

"Do you care?"

"No."

We stood on the sidewalk. I took a deep lungful of the fragrances of Hollywood—the gasoline, the exotic Oriental foods, the perfumes. A gang of Latino punks stood on the corner of Cherokee. I was kind of scared of them, but Zombie waved at them and they waved back.

"Want me to show you the seamy streets?" Zombie said.

"I guess."

"Let's go then."

Probably wasn't the down-home concept of the proper way to go out on a date, but there it was. She held my hand tightly, almost as though she were afraid I'd disappear, and we charged off into the crowd.

CHAPTER 16

I Walked With a Zombie

WE WALKED TOGETHER down the Boulevard. We were together and not together at the same time; what I mean is, even though sometimes her hand skimmed mine, very lightly, those moments were like the intersection of different universes. I wondered if I seemed that way to people. It was the first time that had ever occurred to me. Also sometimes it felt that the two of us were in another universe and like all this color and tacky spectacle around us was outside, like it never touched us. Universes within universes. The kind of thing Ben loved to talk about, and which I had never understood until now.

The section of the Boulevard we were walking down was full of bookstores. My parents' bookstore and Guru Jack's were the only ones I'd ever set foot in other than, you know, shopping mall chains like B. Dalton. There was a humongous one of those too, but we didn't go in. There were bookstores for sci-fi and bookstores for movie mementoes and even book-stores for gay people, which in McDougal they'd never even have imagined possible. We stuffed our-selves with really weird fast food at this place called New Age Junkfood, which was in the shape of a giant flying saucer with a propeller beanie on top. I had a

153

raw tuna, avocado, and watercress on a pH-balanced sesame seed bun and Zombie had a kiwi-and-papaya turnover. She told me that this type of food was called nouvelle cuisine and was like the most up-to-date food you could eat.

"You can easily tell the tourists," Zombie said as we walked down the boulevard. "They're the ones who are always staring at their feet." I'd been scanning the stars embedded in the sidewalk, searching for Tygh's name, but I immediately looked up guiltily. I didn't want anyone to think I was some kind of star-struck bumpkin. "It's not there anyways," she said, reading my mind. "He's like not quite famous enough yet, or he hasn't gone to the right parties, or something."

We walked farther. I marveled at many things: a movie theater built in the shape of an Egyptian temple, humongous old cars that bounced up and down on like these hydraulic devices, and the people, loud and bright and animated. It was an ugly place, really. But behind the brash, peeling, burned-out exterior you could feel the unformed dreams of all these people, dreams waiting to come true. It's a strange feeling to be so fascinated and so repelled at the same time.

"How long have you been into Bloodsucker?" she asked me suddenly.

"Since the game was first delivered to the local arcade," I said. "It's awesome. The local paper did an article about me and that game, did you know that?"

She looked like she was going to say something scornful, but then she changed her mind. I wanted to ask, "What happened to make you act so nice, so normal?" but I didn't want to push my luck too far. The better I knew this girl, the more she seemed a stranger to me. I guess that was what made her attractive to me. A girl like Sissy Pavlat is kind of an open book. When she's mad she rages, when she's sad she cries. She can't help spilling out everything she's thinking.

But this girl was like one of those medieval books I learned about in Mrs. Hulan's social studies class, the ones with padlocks on them. And when Zombie finally tossed me the key, it turned out to be in a foreign language.

I said, "I guess that was my one great moment of fame, the local paper deal. Not much to brag about, but it's all I got."

"It's more than I have," Zombie said, with surprising bitterness.

"You've got to be joking," I said. "You've got all the things my hippie-turned-yuppie parents are always saying they want."

"You play Bloodsucker because it's fun, don't you?"

"Don't you?"

"Nah. I play it and I pretend that I'm the vampire—"

"Well, sure, everyone likes to imagine they're like this bad romantic evil dude—"

"—and that the vampire hunter is my father. That's why I play the game, so I can think about him. And I always hope he catches me."

"Why do you tell terrible stories about him? They're not true, are they?"

"No," she said in a very small voice. "But like, maybe a horrible abusive father is better than one who just like ups and dies on you and you never hear from him again. Until that séance."

At that moment one of those massive old cars with teeth pulled up alongside us. Zombie moved closer to me. She seemed frightened. The window rolled down and I saw this totally ancient old man with white hair. He wore a gold chain and a turquoise shirt with its buttons all undone so you could see his chest, which was mostly ribs and wispy hair. He smiled at us. It was like sort of a grinning skull. I didn't like him, but I thought it was maybe her grandfather or something.

"Hi, Zombie," he said. "Who's your friend?"

"You know this guy?" I said to her.

"I'm busy!" she shouted at him. "Otherwise engaged! Get lost!"

She grabbed my arm so hard it hurt, and yanked me into the thick of the crowd.

"What's the matter?" I said.

"Let's duck in here!" she whispered urgently. "C. C. Brown's got the best ice cream in the universe."

I didn't understand her sudden craving for ice cream but I didn't resist when she shoved me into this sort of 1920s-looking place and ordered a couple of hot fudge sundaes. When they came, I realized that I'd never tasted anything this rich—the toasted almonds, the vanilla, the warm, gooey chocolate—and I kind of sat there, dazed by the sugar high, not quite taking in anything that was happening.

"Who was that?" I said. "Why did you have to escape?"

"Oh, I don't know. An ex-client. I just didn't want to cope at the moment."

I said, "I was hoping that, when you told me what you—I mean, how you earned—I mean—I mean, I was hoping that was another one of your stories."

"Eat your ice cream." Her eyes were far away. I thought of the mask of the madwoman again. I took a long sip of ice water and looked at her, wondering whether these bizarre sensations I was feeling qualified as being in love. What would my parents say if I finally came home and announced, "I'm going to marry a Valley punk hooker"?

I imagined my dad saying something like, "Well, as long as you give each other plenty of personal space, kids." For some reason, it didn't make me mad to think of him saying that about us. I thought it was kind of funny, actually.

Then again, they'd probably argue over chickens, I decided. But was that so bad? The more I thought about that appalling fight in the car on the way to the funeral, the more I began to see that, horrible as it had been, it had its funny side.

The table was narrow and I was sort of fidgeting with my hands and I guess they collided with hers. The next thing I knew she was holding on to my hands real tight and desperate, as though I was her one true hope in her whole messed-up universe. And that was an absurd feeling for her to have, but I could tell how real it was and I felt embarrassed and also terribly powerful because there was someone who needed me and no one else would do. I squeezed her hands back—they were shaking, they were totally cold—and we didn't say anything for a long time because the silence said more than we could say. I mean that we didn't know what we were supposed to say or the thoughts we were supposed to think. So we just sat there. It was the longest we had ever touched each other.

Then she said, "There are some things I keep to myself, you know. I let them touch me in a lot of places, but I never let them kiss me."

I smiled and I leaned across the table and touched her lips lightly with my lips. Just a brief moment. Then I retreated because they were so cold. "It's only from the ice cream," she said, and dabbed at her mouth with a napkin. Then I kissed her again, not minding that the laminated plastic edge of the table-top slammed into my solar plexus and almost knocked me through the wall. She said, "That was like a wonderful gift, J.J. Thanks."

I rubbed my stomach. "You don't know how much that hurt."

"I really like you," she said. I looked into her eyes and thought I saw the mask dissolve a little. "What can I give you that would be as big as what you gave me? God, I'm still all shook up from seeing that guy. You don't know what he's like." She reached into her jacket and found something . . . a small bottle of white plastic, the kind you get headache tablets in. "Here," she said, "I never share this with anyone . . . but you look pretty shook up yourself. We both need to chill out a bit." She kind of hunched up so no one could see over her shoulder and then she poured a small amount of this pink, grainy powder into her hand. Then she sprinkled it over the rest of her sundae. She started to do the same to mine.

"Wait a minute," I said. "What is it?"

"I don't know exactly. Some kind of downers, like I always carry some on me. 'Ludes, maybe."

"These are—" I said.

"Not so loud!"

"Drugs?" I whispered.

"Of course they are, stupid! They're like valuable too, and like this is a big deal, me sharing them with you, so stop acting like such a nerd. Eat your ice cream."

"No." I was real uncomfortable. She obviously thought she was giving me something totally precious.

I didn't want to look like a nerd. I was used to being considered cool and defending my brother from people who called him a nerd. He'd be standing around and staring weirdly ahead and someone would laugh at him and I'd say something like, "Well, he's a genius; what do you expect?"

Or else he'd launch into one of his long-winded, polysyllabic philosophical speeches and I'd try to defuse it by cracking a dumb joke, and he'd stop in midsentence and say to me, "Oh, sorry, J.J. Am I embarrassing you again?"

And I'd smile and say, "Of course not."

It was bogus to have the roles reversed all of a sudden.

"Why not?" I thought. "Mom and Dad used to do dope back in the golden sixties they're always going on and on about." But I couldn't bring myself to eat the ice cream. "No," I said again, trying to avoid sounding like an adult.

"You're no fun. You're like Tygh. He may look and act cool when he's performing, but in real life he's like totally rah-rah. I hate him. He's always trying to run my life. What a phony." She took a bite of ice cream and licked her lips. "See? It's easy."

"No," I said, my voice rising.

"But we've come so far together!" Zombie said. I could see the bewilderment on her face. My reaction must have seemed completely alien to her. "Oh, Dad was right," she said at last. "I have to free myself, no one can do it for me. Not even you."

"I don't think that's what he meant," I said.

"How would you know? You're not my father. You weren't even there. Do you know what he told me? I'm going to do what he says. I'm going to free myself. The only way I can. Forever."

And suddenly I remembered the dream I'd had where I was ferrying the boat and she was the passenger and I was tearing off her mask and finding another mask and another and another . . . and it was almost as if I were back in the dream for one vivid, terrifying moment, and I myself trying to pull the final mask away and finding that it was glued to her face and that it was weeping blood from the eyeholes. . . . I tried to shake the dream loose. I said, "You don't have to obey the voice. It was just a trick, an illusion . . . it was me in the statue, it was my voice. . . ."

"You're lying. You couldn't have known all those things—"

"I did know them." I tried to be gentle. But I was hurting her terribly and I didn't feel like stopping. "I talked to Justin about you. And anyways you're not remembering the most important thing. The voice told you to forget your father. Don't you remember that? That you'd created this demon to hate and that you could destroy the demon all by yourself."

"You're lying!" But I saw that she remembered all of it.

"'Forget me.'" It slipped out in that same voice. It took me by surprise and I whirled around, wildly imagining there might be somebody else at our table.

So maybe it *had* just been me, and not some supernatural spirit possession deal.

She stared at me, then screamed, "You're not my father! I know what my father said, and you're not taking it away from me, do you hear?"

She stood up and flung the rest of her sundae in my face. I flinched and cried out.

"You're just like my brother," she shouted, "you're just like all of them. You're not my father and you never will be and nor will anyone else."

Then she stalked away, leaving me staring at her empty seat through rivulets of dripping chocolate syrup.

I was furious with her and with myself too, because I'd come so close to letting loose of all those emotions inside me. I hadn't meant to do that! I'd tried to help her, hadn't I? Jekyll and Hyde, damn right. She'd come out of her shell for maybe a half hour and then she'd backed right into it again.

"Women!" I said to myself. That was what you were supposed to say after one of these scenes, wasn't it? Ruefully I wiped the chocolate from my eyes. I didn't want to lick the part that was coming down my nose into my mouth in case it was contaminated with those downers.

She had stood me up for her part of the check and I didn't have enough money on me to pay for the two sundaes. I had to call Guru Jack from the store to come over and bail me out.

CHAPTER 17

The Zottoli Mansion

"You are looking awful," the guru said as he handed the cashier his VISA card. "Like you have been seeing a ghost, isn't it? But I have never heard of anyone having a séance in C. C. Brown's before."

"No, that's not it," I said, too confused to explain. "It's just that I'm learning more and more about some people and I don't really like what I'm learning."

"You are seeming a little shook up," Guru Jack said.

"I am, I am," I said.

"You are in a state of karmic imbalance," he said, "and I am thinking that you are requiring something to take your mind off the whole thing, isn't it?"

"Yeah."

Jack bought some more ice cream to take back to the store. "There is nothing like overindulgence," he said, "to correct the balance of karma by bringing everything back through the eternal cycle of being."

Normally I would have laughed but I didn't. As soon as we got back, I flopped down on one of the floor cushions and moped for a long time, while the guru played one of those wailing Indian hit numbers on the store stereo. I guess I felt kind of betrayed. I don't know what I had expected of someone named Zombie McPherson.

After we had some more ice cream, I lay back and stared at the straw matting for a while. It had sort of a hypnotic effect. I found myself counting the little strands of straw, one by one by one. I started fantasizing about being inside a video game . . . inside Bloodsucker . . . with the spiked walls caving in on me. I closed my eyes. A quick memory—Ben reaching out to me—against the trees—the light through the foliage dappling his face. I knew it was a fragment of what I'd blocked from my mind . . . a small piece of the Forgetting Place. I was standing at the very edge of all those memories now. Something about me and Zombie had brought me closer to unlocking the secret. Instinctively I drew away from the memory. I was afraid of the pain. But I wanted to linger there too, to see if I could see another glimpse of what was inside that place.

It was like one of the TV game shows, you know, "curtain number three" and all that . . . and I didn't know whether what was behind the curtain was the jackpot or the booby prize.

When I looked up, Guru Jack was making weird faces at me. I laughed. "Oh, at least I am capable of conjuring up some reaction in you!" he said.

"Huh? Oh, hi."

"You have been sitting there in a transcendental state for several hours," Jack said. "If only I could achieve the same state you have been achieving, I would be a real live, full-time guru instead of having to manage a pretentious bookstore and a sleazy arcade!"

I rubbed my eyes. "How long have I been—"

"Closing time," Jack said.

I looked outside. Daylight was almost gone. Loud

neon signs flashed. I must have been out for hours.

"Hungry?" said the guru abruptly.

"Yeah, kind of."

"Well, I think we need some kind of diversion, isn't it? I do not want you to brood endlessly. Let me see now . . . video games?"

"I don't think so."

"No . . . I think you are getting burned out. Disneyland? But you are too old . . . I have it! We will go to a party."

"A party?"

"Yes . . . you have heard of those extravagant parties they have around here, no? I think there will be one tonight at the house of that producer . . . Zottoli."

"I saw him once," I said, remembering him from the first séance I'd ever witnessed. "You know him?"

"Not exactly. But he is producing one of Tygh's music videos. We are a little bit connected. I am not seeing any reason why we should not be crashing his gate."

"Crashing his gate?" Sometimes I wasn't sure if he was putting on that Indian accent or whether it was just another element of his playacting, fooling with people's minds, you know. "You mean, like, just turn up?" Maybe I'm too strictly brought up or something, but I didn't quite feel right about just showing up at some dude's house.

"Well . . . no shindig like that is complete without at least one guru. As I recall, Zottoli's pet guru, Shri Hanuman, is often present at these affairs in case someone urgently needs spiritual advice. He and I come from rival schools of guruhood, though. You see, he takes himself very seriously, while I am being totally laid back and, as you know, am more into science fiction than fantasy. Well . . . one guru looks

very much like another. I will simply impersonate
him."

"What if he shows up?"

"The more the merrier." He chuckled. "Perhaps we
can entertain our fans with a lively debate on the
finer points of our philosophies."

"What about me?" I felt pretty dubious about this
whole thing, although Jack usually knew what he was
doing even when he pretended to be totally other-
worldly. "How are you going to explain me away to
them?"

"We will figure out something. Now help me close
up the store."

"We will figure out something," indeed! I soon saw
what he had in mind when we reached Aunt Casey's
house. He went upstairs and came down with something that looked like a bed sheet. He told me to take
my clothes off and put on just a pair of shorts.

"Oh, no, you don't!" I said. "I'm not going around
in a sheet."

"Just pretend it's a toga party," he said. "Do not be
a spoilsport!"

I went into the back room. There was a message on
the TV screen waiting for me:

```
WELL, WELL, LITTLE BROTHER, HOW'VE
YOU BEEN? HAS THE WEBB FOUNDATION CON-
TACTED YOU YET? IF YOU START NET-
WORKING WITH THEM, MAYBE WE'LL BE ABLE
TO TALK IN PERSON, FACE TO FACE, IN-
STEAD OF ME LEAVING YOU THESE MESSAGES
ON THIS TIRESOME COMPUTER.
```

There was a flashing cursor, so I was supposed to
press Return for more from my brother. But I just
didn't feel like taking any more of this from a computer right now. I pulled off my T-shirt and threw it over

the screen. I could still see through the thin fabric, so I covered it up with my pants too. All I could see was something flashing at the bottom of the screen as I left the room.

In the kitchen, Jack wrapped me up in the bed sheet. "And now for the dot in the middle of your forehead," he said.

"Hey, like, no makeup," I said.

"No . . . we don't do things that way anymore," he said, reaching into a drawer and pulling out a sheet of adhesive, press-on red dots. He selected one, peeled it off, and smoothed it down on my forehead. "You are wanting to look in a mirror?" he said.

"I don't think so. Do I really have to go like this?"

"It is more fun this way."

I sighed and rolled my eyes.

It was dark—maybe nine o'clock or so—when Guru Jack and I and his many-colored gurumobile arrived at the party. I was nervous when we left Aunt Casey's, even more nervous when the guru turned uphill into one of those scenic canyon routes and we started whizzing against gravity . . . even more when we started coasting down Mulholland Drive and the guru took his hands off the wheel and began reciting a mantra. Suddenly I noticed that his foot wasn't on the accelerator or the brake. In fact, he was sitting cross-legged on the seat, and there was a humongous book holding down the pedal. In fact . . . I wasn't quite sure if his eyes were open or not . . . "Hey, like, slow down!" I screamed. He didn't seem to notice. We were rushing downhill with a curve coming up and about to smash into a rock—

I grabbed the wheel and we barely missed getting crushed to a pulp.

"Oh, thank you," the guru said, coming to and

putting his hands back on the wheel. "I think you will be good at drag racing when you will be getting your driver's license."

"You nearly got us killed!" I shouted at him.

"I knew you would react in time," he said. "Oh, I had better be slowing down now, I think we are arriving." He started to unfold his legs. He seemed to take forever just to lower his feet to the floor.

We screeched to a stop and turned into a tiny street that snaked around these great big palms, and then this awesome like Arabian Nights-type palace was poking out of the side of the hill.

Every car pulling into the driveway of the Zottoli mansion seemed to be a hundred miles long and gleaming. Every car that wasn't like a Rolls was a Ferrari or a Bugatti, and these uniformed dudes were directing anything that didn't look impressive to park somewhere outside the gates. "Better go to the left and park behind," I said. "We won't be as conspicuous."

"Guru Jack is not a second-class citizen," he said, and pulled up right behind one of the monster limousines. A dude tried to motion us away, but Jack pretended not to notice. At last the doorman came down the steps and opened the door.

"Oh, it's the guru," the man said. "I guess it's okay." Another, more impressively uniformed dude was peering out from behind these humongous columns, like in a Roman temple.

Jack handed me a tambourine that he kept in the glove compartment and said, "Start banging away before they start complaining." He got a tambourine for himself, and a basket of what looked like shredded flowers.

"Excuse me, sir," the more impressive dude was saying, "I know Mr. Zottoli is expecting you, but maybe you ought to park—"

I pounded hard on the instrument and it jangled, making the impressive dude jump. He started to protest some more, but I drowned him out. Then Guru Jack began chanting away in a weird, high-pitched singsong. "Just do what I do," he said under his breath as the startled doormen let us in. I started wailing along with him. I guess I did a pretty good job, because no one questioned me or stopped me. It was probably because I had heard so much of Jack's music blaring over the loudspeakers at the store. He and I were dancing up a storm and I barely had time to take in the spectacle in front of us because of all the racket I was making.

We were in a hallway lined with marble and bronze statues of naked men and women with their arms spread out in various uncomfortable positions. Wandering among the statues were these people. Some of them were wearing tuxedos and long evening dresses like at the Oscars and others were wearing casual clothes, faded jeans and such, although I suspected that they were the kind of jeans that you paid an extra hundred dollars to have them specially made to look all dirty and worn out, not jeans that got worn out naturally. At the opposite end of the hall were open French windows, and I could hear splashing sounds from beyond. I guess there must have been a pool there.

More people in impressive uniforms were going around, noses and trays held stiffly in the air. I didn't dare stop the singing and dancing in case someone tried to talk to me. I recognized the star of a TV sitcom reclining on some zebra skins that were piled against one wall. There were other people I half recognized . . . the kind of people you see in American Express commercials but you never know who they are.

"Stay casual," the guru said in my ear. "Don't stare at everyone or they'll know we're crashing the party." He danced around a little more. I saw that he was dancing very purposefully, moving in one particular direction . . . toward the pool deck beyond the French windows.

I followed him. People were laughing at us but not shooing us away. I guess they had us figured for part of the entertainment. Outside, there was this Olympic-size pool, and beyond it a Jacuzzi big enough for about twenty or thirty people, with like another of those statues rising from the middle, a nude lady standing in a giant seashell.

Next to the Jacuzzi was a floodlit table piled high with food. A couple of chefs were standing behind it, dishing it out. It was all weird food like what they served at New Age Junkfood. There was a sculpture of a sci-fi spaceship—I recognized it from a movie preview I'd seen, and I wondered if it was one of Zottoli's films.

"Okay, kid," the guru said. "We have penetrated far enough. No more need for singing. Time instead for eating." He grabbed my arm and dragged me to the table. Then he took a plate and started helping himself. "Yes," he said, pointing at one of the chefs, "a few slices of the smoked salmon . . . a little more . . . yes, just one more . . . perhaps another . . . it is so helpful to my meditations, you know."

It was all so ridiculous, I couldn't control my giggling.

"Quick! Eat something fast!" He shoved something into my mouth so I'd stop laughing. I almost choked on it. It tasted pretty good, though.

I made a questioning gesture as I tried to swallow the squishy, garlicky lump.

"Snails," he said.

I didn't know if he was having me on, but it was too late to throw up now. I was doomed to enjoy yet another weird gourmet delicacy.

I heard someone shouting at us from the Jacuzzi. "Ah, Hanuman!" It was Zottoli; I recognized him from the séance. He was in the tub, surrounded by three or four beautiful women who were like bobbing up and down beside him.

"Totally awesome," the guru said, raising his arms in a posture of blessing.

"Oh, no," I said, terrified that the producer would realize that Jack was the wrong guru. But there was like so much steam rising from the Jacuzzi, or else Zottoli was so drunk, that he didn't seem to notice.

At that moment, however, the sound of more tambourines and wailing came across the pool. "Eat fast," the guru said to me. "Every bite may be your last." I started munching furiously on the snails. Jack was trying to stuff an entire side of smoked salmon into his saffron robe. He saw me gawking and said, "I am thinking we might be needing midnight snack."

At that moment, dozens of drum-beating dotheads burst into the pool area. "Maybe we can slip away," I said.

"They are standing in the way," Jack whispered.

"How about out through the back?"

"Yes," he said. "Quick. Follow me."

Too late! There was another guru marching across the deck, his finger pointed at Jack, shouting, "In the name of Krishna, an impostor!"

"I guess I'll just have to be toughing this out," Jack said. He started pointing at the other guru dude, and they started screaming bizarre curses at each other.

"Try to get away!" he said to me between rounds of insults. "Find the car . . . start it . . . I'll be out as soon as I can . . . keys in my sandal . . . you misinformed offspring of a demented camel!" He stepped out of his flip-flops, and I saw a set of car keys. I swooped down to grab them and headed toward the back.

I slipped through a clump of perfectly groomed bushes onto this lawn beyond the pool, which was about the size of the entire McDougal High School baseball field. It was dark except for these bizarre modern sculptures which were all illuminated with like these coiled neon lights, each one in a floodlit pool. There were people all over the lawn.

"Oh, J.J.—" I recognized the man from the Webb Foundation. He was sitting on a little Persian rug at the base of one of those modern sculptures which was in the shape of sort of a pregnant pyramid with like monsters trying to claw their way out. A bunch of others were with him. I recognized Caressa Byrd, the romance novelist, from the first séance I'd observed, and there were also a couple of "high-punk" types with the Krazy Glue rainbow hair.

I tried to get away, but he said, "Not so fast, young man! Isn't it exhilarating? We're so close to the ultimate truth!"

"Let me go," I said.

"We've set the date for the next big networking," the man said, "this coming Sunday, midnight. We still need a couple of sensitives . . ."

"You already tested me and I was useless," I said. "Please leave me alone—"

"I'm sure your brother would have wanted you to—" His eyes were all glassy, like a zombie's. I wondered if he had been taking any drugs.

Caressa Byrd laughed, a wild, crazy laugh, like the

cackling of a cartoon witch. I had to get away . . . I had to!

"Come Saturday midnight, there'll be magic . . . mysterious forces will be let loose over the world . . . we will see glimpses of other universes . . . we will know the future . . . imagine the glory of it! If we can only show people the truth of what is to come . . . we could take away the terror of uncertainty . . . people would be truly happy for the first time. Wouldn't they?"

"I don't know!" I said.

"Exactly," he said. "If you did know, you would feel much better. . . ."

I turned to avoid talking to him anymore. Suddenly I saw—I thought I saw—Zombie McPherson. She was deep in conversation with this totally old dude —looked sort of like a skeleton—in a pool of light under the next statue along. At first I was surprised, then I realized that it was probably no big deal for her to turn up at these parties. The two of them didn't see me because I had ducked into the darkness.

I crept up real close to them and hid behind a curvy section of the sculpture. They were talking real intensely, in whispers, and I couldn't quite hear what they were saying.

She looked terrible. I thought that it might have been because of something I'd said in the ice cream parlor. Her eyes were sunken. Her skin seemed so pale you could almost see through it. And she was shaking something fierce. And crying, I think, because her face was streaked and moist. At last she said something like, "The guesthouse." She forced a wan smile from her lips. The old dude kind of snorted and walked away into the shadows.

Zombie started to follow.

I called her name softly. It was warm and the sound

of crickets filled the air. She turned. She looked at me. It was like she only half recognized me. "What do you want?" she said. Her speech was slurred and she was shaking harder now.

She hugged her leather jacket hard to her chest, even though it was so hot.

"Are you cold?" I said. Suddenly I didn't know what else to say. The scene we'd gone through earlier that day weighed so heavily in my mind that I didn't dare bring it up.

She said, "Please leave me alone." And her voice was like an echo of my own. I mean, it reminded me of me trying to get rid of all those dudes who had been invading my grief over Ben's death. It really threw me and I didn't know what to say again.

I said, "Listen, I'm sorry I reacted like that. I mean, who am I to make judgments about you? It's your life, not mine. I don't do drugs and I never will and I don't think you ought to but I shouldn't have like panicked when I saw what you had . . . I had this one image of how you are and I tricked myself into thinking it was all true. But it wasn't." I knew what I was saying was true but maybe it didn't have anything to do with anything anymore.

Maybe she heard me and maybe she didn't. She still didn't seem to recognize me. "Are you coming to the guesthouse too?" she said, and giggled. Her eyes were totally empty. Like the eyes of the mask of the madwoman.

"No," I said.

"I'll be good, real good," she said, and slowly licked her thin lips.

"Zombie—"

There was a glimmer in her eyes. I think she recognized me at that moment, because she cried out, "You can't see me like this, it's not your world, you don't belong, go back to Kansas!"

I reached out to touch her but she flinched violently away and slipped out of the pool of light. I followed. She was hurrying. I felt her desperation. Again it seemed to echo my own. I saw where she was heading. It was a cottage on the grounds. It stood against the tall stucco wall that ringed the Zottoli estate. There was a red light on inside. It made the cottage look menacing, kind of like it was standing in a pool of blood.

She was really sprinting and I didn't want to look as though I were chasing her, so I lagged behind. I had totally forgotten about the dueling gurus back at the main house. "There's got to be some way I can reach her," I thought. "There's got to be something I can do."

I reached the house. I heard a door slamming somewhere inside. The front door was ajar so I stepped in without thinking of whether I had any right to be there. My foot hit something hard and I stifled a cry. It was a bunch of weight-lifting gear. I stopped and looked around. I didn't see anyone. The front room was boiling hot and I saw Zombie's leather jacket lying on the floor along with some other clothes. A naked red bulb hung from the ceiling and there was like a lot of steam. It came from an open door marked "sauna." I knew what that was because on TV you always get to see rich health freaks in their saunas, sweating away their excess pounds.

I waited around for a while. At last I heard voices coming from inside the sauna. I tiptoed up to the door. The doorway was full of steam and there was very little light, so I couldn't be seen.

"Come on, baby." It was a man's voice, rasping, tired-sounding. "I have what you want . . . you have what I want."

"First you deliver. Then I deliver." It was Zombie's voice. I'd never heard her sound this hard before.

"Can I trust you?"

"I'm a professional."

"You're just an addict, a desperate addict. I despise you."

"The feeling is mutual."

As my eyes grew used to the light, I saw them both. They were squatting on a wooden bench. Steam was billowing everywhere. One of them was the old man I had seen Zombie with earlier. I couldn't see clearly. But I saw her forearm, which had like a handkerchief tied around it. And it was all covered with tiny marks like mosquito bites. She was shaking even worse than before. There was a hypodermic needle on the seat.

I stepped back and stumbled over something. She looked up. She saw me but didn't speak.

"What was that noise?" the old man said. "Did you tell anyone?"

"No." It was just a whimper.

She continued to look at me. Suddenly it was as if I had torn away the madwoman's mask . . . to see the pain beneath it.

"No one can feel so much pain," I thought. It was like she was being sucked into a whirlpool of darkness and she didn't even want to resist anymore, she just wanted to stop feeling anything.

And I knew what the whirlpool of darkness was . . . because I was carrying my own kind of darkness within me. A darkness I dared not look into . . . because I was scared that once I stepped in I would never want to step out again . . . a forgetting place.

And I said very softly, "We all have forgetting places inside ourselves." I don't think she heard me.

I couldn't bear to look. I turned and ran. Ran back to the pool area where the party was in full swing and where both gurus, apparently reconciled, were boogying up a storm together.

When Jack saw me, he sensed that something was wrong and came after me. I didn't care that people were staring, I just wanted to leave that terrible place. We got out of there somehow and I couldn't wait to get back into the car and on the road.

We didn't talk until we hit the freeway. The windows were down and the wind was blasting my face. Finally, he said very gently, "And I was having so much fun." It wasn't a reproach—I think he was just trying to lighten my black mood—but the idea that I had spoiled his evening was the last straw and I found myself just bawling my guts out, just like a little kid.

"There, there," Jack said softly.

"She's a heroin addict or something, I don't know what," I said. "And there's nothing I can do!"

The guru put his arm around my shoulder and I just went on crying. I didn't even care about the side of salmon he'd stashed in his robe that kind of slithered out onto the front seat.

He said, "This is the first time since your brother's death, isn't it? The first time you've cried."

I knew he was right. I just went on crying.

I heard him murmuring on, not really listening to the words but feeling good that someone was there with me: "The first time you've cried . . . that you have allowed something to touch you. I mean your heart. These tears are the beginning of your journey home."

"I'm never going home," I said fiercely. "Never, never." And went on sobbing.

"Not yet, anyway. At least not until after the Senseless Vultures concert, isn't it?"

I was so miserable I didn't even smile.

CHAPTER 18

Not Human Hearts in Aspic

MY T-SHIRT STILL hung over the television screen and any fresh messages from Ben. I made no move to pull it off that night. I just didn't want to watch the screen and see how my dead brother had predicted my latest fiasco. And that was a strange thing, because I had never considered wanting to hide something from him before. Now that he wasn't around, I guess my keeping secrets from him was a totally illogical idea. But he still felt alive to me.

I didn't even have time for nightmares that night. I didn't even fall asleep. All I could think about was Zombie McPherson. I wasn't sure if I loved her or anything like that, but I knew that there were new kinds of feelings in me . . . feelings I didn't know I had . . . feelings that maybe Ben might never have understood.

I lay in bed staring at the ceiling until dawn. I didn't think of the river or the cemetery or the ferryman or the tarot cards. . . .

The next day I sat around the house. Aunt Casey left me alone; she sensed I wasn't ready to talk, and she didn't ask any questions. Around four in the afternoon, though, I wandered into the kitchen and raided the refrigerator. The side of salmon, which I had last

177

seen on the floor of Guru Jack's car, was now sitting elegantly on a blue and white porcelain platter. It didn't look at all dirty, so I sliced off a hunk of it and ate it. I searched for something to drink and ended up pouring myself something green from a bottle marked *kombucha*. It tasted like liquid seaweed. I guess that's what it was.

"What will you wear to the concert?" Aunt Casey asked me. She had come in unnoticed, silent as a ninja.

The concert had slipped my mind. How was that possible? Only a week ago I would have considered a Senseless Vultures concert the most important thing in the whole world. "I guess I kind of forgot," I said.

"We just got a call from your friend Tygh. He is sending Justin to pick us up. You are a very important guest. You must have done something right for him."

"He thinks I really helped his sister. But I think he's wrong, I don't think anyone can save her."

"You don't want to talk about it?"

"I want to. But I just can't."

She seemed to accept that. That was what I liked most about her. She never hurried me and she never chewed me out for trying to work something out by myself.

At last I said, "Is it okay if I like don't go to the concert?" But even as I said that, I knew that would be the wrong thing to do. Because I was getting the feeling that my facing the problem of Zombie Mc-Pherson was somehow tied in with locating and coming to terms with the Forgetting Place.

I don't mean I was falling for the guru's shtick about everything in the universe being somehow connected to everything else—I mean, this was real life, and Guru Jack wasn't Yoda and for sure I wasn't Luke Skywalker.

But all the things I had learned seemed to be converging on some kind of Big Truth. This Big Truth is something that everyone seems to chase after a lot. Maybe it's an illusion. I wanted to find out for myself, not wait for some prepackaged version of it to come my way. That seemed to be the right way to pursue this thing.

I wanted to tell all that to Zombie, and I figured Zombie would be at the concert. Maybe she wouldn't be totally wasted, and maybe we could start all over again from scratch. Because in spite of how confused this was making me, I knew that I liked her a lot and I hoped I could help her somehow. And my relationship to her was something completely mine that I didn't have to share with anyone else, not my brother, not my parents, not any of my friends.

It was best to stay casual and let whatever was going to happen happen and stop brooding about it.

So I went to my room to see what I could wear. I knew there wasn't much, but I didn't want to look totally retarded.

I found a note taped to the bed that hadn't been there before. It said, "Look under the mattress!"

"What the hell," I said to myself, and pried loose the bed sheet. I gasped. Hidden there were like the most radical clothes I had ever seen, all black and red and chrome, the kind of thing people wear in sci-fi movies. I had never had clothes like this before because Mom and Dad weren't into, you know, show-off external things. It was something from the sixties that they still believed in. It was strange how, in their climb to respectable near-yuppiehood, they had given up everything that was fun about the sixties and kept only the bad parts. Well, at least almost everything. I mean, some of the other kids at McDougal had it really rough . . . their parents didn't let them do anything or wouldn't discuss sex with them or weren't straight with them in other ways. I guess Mom and Dad always did try to be open with Ben and me, when they could, not to lie to us.

I gave my parents only a moment's thought, because I had to put on all the radical clothes and then go into the bathroom and see myself in all my glory and I was awesome.

I was still admiring my totally casual splendor when Justin Casper arrived and it was time to go to the Nelson Pavilion, which is a glittering, brand-new place halfway up the Santa Monica Mountains. It is all glass and chrome and, though it's completely enclosed and air-conditioned, it seems to have no walls and you seem suspended over the Valley with the view that goes on and on over the infinitely shrinking lattice of city lights.

We parked in this special VIP parking lot and Justin took us in through an underground passageway that kept branching off.

"I'd never find my way out of here," I said. I'd brought the CD Walkman with me, because I wanted to immerse myself totally in the Vultures' music even before I saw them live. I wanted so much to drown myself in the blasting music. If it was loud enough, I wouldn't feel confused anymore. I wouldn't feel anything except the rhythm, pounding, pounding.

He walked briskly and Guru Jack, Aunt Casey, and I had a hard time following him. We seemed to be going uphill for a while, and then we emerged in this like private viewing box that hung out over the front of the stage. There was music from the stage that didn't blend with the sound on my CD. I turned it down. It wasn't the Vultures but a warm-up band —kind of bland actually—doing some kind of love ballad. They were all dressed as circus clowns. It was amusing to watch their moves, but the music was totally dull so I didn't pay much attention to it. Just above my head I could see all these catwalks and lights and all sorts of stage props on wires ready to be dropped down. Above the catwalks there were like these pipes and tubes and stuff, and above that, in the ceiling, some square vents.

There were about a half-dozen chairs in the box —easy chairs, not the cramped theater seats like the regular audience. And a coffee table, a wet bar, even a few trays of snacks. Behind the bar there was a grille, about as tall and wide as me, and behind that I could see a narrow shaft that seemed to lead upward with some rungs for climbing. Ventilation ducts, probably. Probably they were somehow connected to the vents in the ceiling, way above the stage.

This warm-up band wasn't bad, but I got the feeling something was wrong after they'd been playing for almost an hour. I looked out over the audience and saw that they weren't really getting into the mood at all—they looked restless. There were only a few people jumping up and down in the aisles. I asked Guru Jack what time it was.

"Almost nine-thirty."

"They've been playing for like an hour and a half, two hours, and Tygh's group hasn't even come on yet," I said. "What a rip-off! The audience seems to know it too."

"I think they have been repeating themselves," Jack said. I hadn't really been listening. I couldn't tell. Actually I'd been steadily turning up the Vultures album on my CD player, and it was at least as loud as the warm-up band's playing, so I'd have to say that my ears were pretty fried. Only Aunt Casey seemed to be having a good time. She was like wiggling her head from side to side like one of those Indian temple dudes.

Suddenly Tygh came charging into the viewing box.

"What's happening?" I had to shout to hear myself.

He tore off my headphones and said, "Can't you see? Up there . . . above the catwalk . . ."

All I could see were those ceiling vents I had seen earlier. Then the spotlights shifted, following one of the clown costume dudes, and I thought I saw something move. Inside the vent opening. Something pale and limber and . . . with a Mohawk.

"Oh, my God," I said softly to myself.

"She's gonna jump, I swear she's gonna jump." Tygh was keeping out of the view of the audience. I squinted, not trusting my eyes. "She left a note in my dressing room." I saw that he had no makeup on, and that he wasn't wearing one of the space age or medieval or Japanese costumes that the group was famous for. All he had on were faded jeans and a shirt that said, "My parents went to Mars and all I got was this lousy T-shirt."

All I could say was, "Ben."

"I can't do anything!" Tygh said. "She's crawling through the vents. Only a scrawny kid could get up there—"

I can't describe the anguish on his face. But I knew those feelings well. They were the same feelings I had denied myself all this time. The feelings I'd pushed into my personal forgetting place. But there was something about him that made me really mad. I looked into his eyes and it looked to me like he was thinking, "I've already lost her, she's gone, it's no use."

"Can't you do something?" I said accusingly.

"I've called the fire department," he said. I watched

the tiny figure as the spotlight shifted again. Her face was pale, so pale. She had painted dark circles around her eyes. It looked like she was trying to lower herself out of the vent.

Tygh showed me her note. It said, "Don't you dare send someone along the catwalk to pry me loose. I'll stay here till I'm ready and then I'm going to jump." Then it said, "Thank J.J.'s brother for showing me the way."

When I saw those words I think I screamed. I didn't care who could hear me. "She's got no right to blame it on Ben. She's got no right to drag me into this—" That's the awful thing. I didn't feel a great urge to rush out and save her. What I felt was more like, "How dare she do this to me!" She'd betrayed me. That's what she'd done! I was so angry I could barely see. There was like this red cloud bursting in front of my eyes.

I must have screamed pretty damn loud because I think someone in one of the front rows heard me and looked up . . . and then it was too late because they'd spotted Tygh . . . and they started chanting his name over and over: *Tygh! Tygh! Tygh! Tygh! Tygh! Tygh!* They wanted him, they wanted him on that stage that minute. The rhythm of it pounded my ears and engulfed the clowns on stage. They must have felt totally retarded.

Tygh looked down at his fans. The roaring was a hungry thing, a bloodthirsty thing. I guess I'd always thought that celebrities love the thrill of being worshiped more than anything in the world. I mean, when you dream about being rich and famous, you dream about thousands of people shrieking out your name, loving you, demanding you. But I didn't see any of that in Tygh's face. What I saw was more like . . . fear, maybe. Certainly resignation.

"There's nothing I can do," he said. So terribly softly. I didn't hear it, I just read his lips.

"I guess I didn't help at all." I didn't tell him I'd found out about the drugs. I guess he knew all along.

"Sure you helped."

He put his arm around my shoulder and led me out into the passageway. It was only slightly quieter there. He said, "I've done everything I can. I guess it wasn't enough. I'm not her father and I can't ever be."

I was still angry at her. I thought about how I'd cried my guts out last night. It had been for nothing. She was going to walk out of my life. Just like Ben. I hated her. I hated him too. I hated my brother. It felt good to hate him.

"The show has to go on," Tygh said. And he started to walk away from me.

"What? You're going to go out there and . . ."

"The world isn't going to stop and wait for my heart to finish breaking."

"She's doing just what my brother did to me," I said. "I hate them, I hate them."

"No." His lips barely moved.

I said, "You're not even trying to stop her."

He looked at me, helpless, pathetic. My idol. My hero. A wimp. He didn't say anything. He'd already lost the battle, he was giving up. I hated him. I hated everyone.

The crowd was screaming and swaying like sharks in a feeding frenzy. Far, far in the background I could hear a siren.

"I'm not going to let her do it, do you hear?" I didn't quite know what I was going to do. I watched him as he hurried down the corridor. Then I marched back into the viewing box. Resolutely I put my headphones back on and turned up the music. Aunt Casey and Jack were staring at me. I guess I must have looked like I'd gone off the deep end or something. I went over to the ventilation grille and started to work it free. I was damn well going to find Zombie and yank her away from the brink before she could mess up Tygh's life the way Ben had messed up mine. No, she wasn't messing up Tygh's life. Tygh had given up. It was *my* life she was messing up. Her and Ben and everyone else I'd ever tried to care about.

I pushed on into the shaft. I didn't even know if I could reach Zombie that way. But I'm not a big kid and if anyone could do it I could.

As soon as I was in the shaft I couldn't breathe. There was a choking smell, some kind of chemical. I felt like a plunger in a stopped-up toilet bowl. The passageway sloped gently upward, so even though there weren't any toeholds, I was able to work myself farther and farther along. The walls were metal, cold against my cheeks and palms. It occurred to me that I might never be able to get out of there again. "Wandering forever in the Twilight Zone and all that," I told myself, trying to laugh.

I had to go on. It wasn't that I didn't want out. It was just that there wasn't any room in the tunnel to turn around in.

And it was getting darker and darker.

When I turned off the CD, I could still hear the crowd. Actually, the whole shaft was vibrating from their roaring. Somehow the ducts acted as a natural amplifier. I could hear the music, too. It was muffled by the sound of the crowd. This faint, the songs of the dancing clowns didn't sound so bad. Still bland, though. I went on. Suddenly the music stopped altogether and the crowd seemed to get louder, louder, louder until my eardrums were like going to burst.

Then there was silence.

And, in the distance, a patch of light.

I wasn't going uphill anymore. I had reached the ceiling. There were passages branching off every which way, but only one of them had the light, flickering on and off every few seconds . . . it must be the spotlight as it tracked someone across the stage.

And then I saw her dimly. She was kneeling at the edge of one of the openings. She hadn't seen me yet. She seemed to be speaking to someone. Maybe there was a dude out on the catwalk trying to talk her into easing herself gently down. . . .

A few soft chords, an intro. Then, all at once, a song I recognized: "Not Human Hearts in Aspic." I couldn't believe that Tygh had actually gone on stage. But it was true. And the song was wild as ever.

I got right behind Zombie. I looked down too. It was Justin on the catwalk. He was making signs. She was shouting down at him: "Get out, get out!"

Then she leaned forward.

I didn't stop to think. I just reached out and grabbed. She turned around and kind of slugged me in the jaw but I held on tight. There was no color in her face at all. I tried to keep my balance. If I fell, I might be able to grab the catwalk in time but I might crack my skull on the stage below, too. I held on to her. I tried not to think of how far down it was.

"You too?" she said when I wouldn't let go. "But you saw the way I am. You know it's not worth going on."

"Go ahead!" I shouted, shaking her urgently. "You don't care how much you're hurting him, do you? Or me."

"You're not supposed to see me cry," she said. The tears spurted down her cheeks. "Go back to Kansas." She seemed tired, so tired. Like she was a thousand years old. "What do you care? You hate me anyways."

"Yeah," I said bitterly. "Guess I do." Because at that moment I was seething with hate for everything and everyone. "Not as much as you hate yourself," I said at last.

"Gag me! Fucking Ann Landers."

"Go ahead, make fun of me," I said. I didn't let go. "You thought you'd just fake my father's voice and order me to forget him and then I'd turn normal, didn't you? And all my problems would like disappear."

"Of course not—I didn't even know—I mean, maybe there—" I was floundering.

"Let me go, damn it! You can't stop me, you don't have any right to."

"Prudie—" It sort of slipped out. I hadn't wanted her to know I knew her real name. Maybe it was because I wasn't thinking straight. I swear, though, it just came out of my mouth and when I'd said it I wished I could have bitten off my tongue.

She twisted free and just stared at me, just stared, wild-eyed. "Who told you that was my name?" she said. "I'm about to commit suicide and all you can do is make fun of my name? Did Tygh tell you, just now, to give you more ammunition against me?"

"I've known it for more than a week."

That sunk in slowly. "I can't believe you never mentioned it."

"It didn't seem to matter."

"Yeah, it matters. Names are everything. You know why I picked the name Zombie? Because I think I'm one of the living dead, you know? Now I can be one of the dead dead. Awesome, huh."

"Prudie's not such a bad name. Hardly worth killing yourself over. It could be worse. You could be named Jeremiah Johnson."

"Jeremiah Johnson . . . no, really! Ha, ha, ha!"

"Stop making fun of me! I can't believe last night I was actually crying for you! I never even cried for Ben."

"That's dumb . . . I'm nothing to you . . . I'm not your brother."

"Bullshit! You don't know what you are to me. You'll never know how I feel until you stop thinking about your stupid self!"

She stared at me. I thought, "I've really done it now, I've made her mad. Now she'll jump just to spite me." But I just said, very softly, because I didn't seem to have any anger left anymore, "It's no use my crying. Or trying to hold you back. Only you can step away."

She made no noise at all for a couple of heartbeats. I thought she was going to jump then, honestly I did. And I made no move to stop her. Because if it was what she wanted, what right did I have to prevent it? Was it going to bring my brother back from the grave? That's what flashed through my mind . . . an image of blood and earth and dead leaves . . . I remembered something else for the first time.

The sound of a gun going off as I stood at the edge of the river gazing upward at the clear Kansas sky.

The mud seeping into my sneakers as I ran into the woods.

Blood oozing between my fingers.

Ben's eyes . . .

I hardly heard what Zombie was saying to me. I was dimly aware that the music had shifted, that the Vultures were playing a new song that I hadn't heard before: a song of long, arching melodies over slow shifting chords and the synthesized whisper of a swift stream. "It's all very well you telling me to step away," she said. "Maybe you've never seen death the way I have. It seduces you. You think death is like totally gross or something but it can be a very beautiful thing. I always wanted something I could love that would love me back. I had a fantasy that my dad was my boyfriend. But like, he was really dead, you know? So then instead I dreamed that death itself was like my lover, and that he'd take me out dancing and I'd feel his bony hands around my waist and I'd kiss his grinning skull." She seemed in another world.

But I had seen death and it wasn't beautiful. It was senseless and messy and ugly and I hated it more than anything in the world. But it was where Ben was, and it called to me in Ben's voice: "Come to me, little brother."

And only a tiny part of me still wanted to resist.

"Help me," I said.

But all she said was, "Only you can step away."

For the first time I saw that what she'd said to me the first time we met was true: "You're just like me." We were alike, she and I. We had both been drawn to the edge of the Forgetting Place.

"You really knew my name the whole time?" she said at last. "You know something? I used to think I'd die if someone knew I was called Prudie. But like, it really doesn't bother me at all. Not at all. I'm not dead. You can call me Prudie if you like."

"Let's get out of here. This is too cramped." Suddenly I noticed that Justin, still waving frantically to us from the catwalk, had been joined by other people —some of them looked like firemen—who were trying to set up a ladder. I poked my head out and made signs to show, "It's okay. We're coming." Justin was so relieved he burst out in a silly grin and started to jump up and down. "It looks like he's actually breakdancing on the catwalk," I said to Zombie. "If I didn't know better—"

She crouched over the opening and peered down.

"He really is," she said. "But that thing's only a couple of feet wide! He'll fall!"

The top of the ladder was bobbing up and down in the vent. I grabbed it and pushed it against the side to steady it. As Zombie and I climbed down to the catwalk, I noticed all these radical objects hanging on wires all around us: castle walls, furniture, trees and shrubs, painted clouds. "Look at all this awesome stuff!" I said.

"Just props," Justin said. "They lower them onto the stage whenever—" There was a whole army of firemen and medical dudes up there with us too. One of them was waving a hypodermic needle, a tranquilizer probably. Another was holding out something that looked like a straitjacket.

"She's not crazy anymore," I said. "You can leave her alone."

The song I'd never heard before was building up to a climax. Beneath the throbbing of the music I could hear the crowd sighing . . . the whole catwalk seemed to vibrate with it.

There was this one cloud suspended beside us. Big, fluffy, and with kind of a big padded seat in the front. "What's that for?"

"Oh, they're setting up for the Shakespeare festival next week," Zombie said.

"Do you think—"

"Come on!"

We kind of clambered onto the seat. Justin looked like he was about to go crazy again. "Hey, like I'm not going to do it, okay?" Zombie said, rolling her eyes. It felt weird just hanging up there. The thing had a big seat belt so it was kind of like strapping yourself into a ride at the amusement park. It was kind of scary when I looked down and saw the stage clearly for the first time since I'd been crawling around the ventilation system.

The whole stage was like a river. There were these rippling lights, deep blue and purple, shot through here and there with laser sparkles. There was fog, everywhere, like in my dream, and a boat drifting through the mist . . . like my dream. But I wasn't afraid.

On the boat stood Tygh Simpson. He was dressed sort of like an alien samurai, and he was wearing a mask like the mask in the book: expressionless, coldly beautiful. I couldn't understand the words of the song: it was like all their other songs, only a word hear and there, but now and then, in the refrain, I thought I heard *Benjamin . . . Bhakti . . . Madigan.* Was I imagining it? I didn't have time to think, because the cloud we were sitting on jerked abruptly and I heard a screech above us, like a badly oiled hinge, and suddenly I realized we were being slowly lowered onto the stage.

One of the stagehands was running along the walk, waving his hands at us and shouting, "Come off of there!" But behind him I saw Justin, kind of chuckling to himself.

"I guess it wasn't the Shakespeare festival after all," Zombie said, as the cloud to our left descended through veils of purple vapor. "Our turn. Let's make it good."

"I guess we should."

So I put my arms around her and kissed her with all my might. At first she was completely unyielding, and I might as well have been kissing a punk Venus de Milo, but about a third of the way down she seemed much softer somehow. The song was coming to an end and the crowd was cheering and the stage lights were so blinding that I had to close my eyes and so did she. We entered our own secret universe. We were in front of thousands of people but we didn't care. We were like in a whole 'nother universe.

The cloud landed—it wasn't gentle, it was with a shuddering thud that knocked us back to planet earth—and we were next to Tygh's boat. The audience was going mad. Tygh came up to us. I couldn't read his face because he was still wearing the mask. Then he spoke. His voice was electronically distorted and rolled through the auditorium like thunder. "I wrote this song for you, J.J. I call it 'Crossing the River.'"

But I hardly heard him. I hardly saw anything because of how brilliant the stage lights were. And the roar of the crowd was deafening. We stood up and slowly, in a daze, walked off stage.

"Thank you," she said. And squeezed my hand, so gently, as if she were afraid of damaging it.

"Yeah," I said.

"I guess it was wrong of me to use your brother as like an excuse or something. I mean, I didn't even know him. He wasn't showing me the way to anywhere."

It was the last time we ever mentioned the subject.

We sat out the rest of the concert in a dressing room backstage. There were several TV monitors so we could watch the concert. But maybe we were more interested in each other than in the music. We didn't talk much, but our silence seemed to say everything we needed to say.

I got a glimpse of Tygh in one of the monitors, running through the corridor to another dressing room. His face was drenched with sweat and he seemed a thousand years old. There was no way I'd ever understand what he must have gone through out there. I was still angry at him, unspeakably angry, because he hadn't done anything to stop Zombie.

Zombie got up to go to him. She wanted me to come too.

"No!" I said. "He would have let you die!"

"He was just scared," Zombie said, and left me.

I knew there were things that only he and she could share. I don't know what went on between them. Maybe they had a big fight, maybe a mushy reconciliation. Whatever it was, at least they had started to speak to each other. And I had helped make it happen. I just sat and waited for her to come back. When she did, she had a shy smile on her lips that I had never seen before.

"Coming to the party?" she said. "There's like a small gathering at the house, just a few friends."

"No," I said. I wasn't ready to forgive Tygh yet.

"Well then, I guess I'll just go with you."

"Nowhere to go."

"Don't care."

She rode back to Burbank with me and Aunt Casey and the guru.

"See you tomorrow," she said to me at the door.

"Tomorrow," I said.

Then I went inside, feeling light-headed and wired. It's not every day that you come floating down into the middle of a rock concert, on a cloud, in the arms of the sister of a totally famous celebrity. And that famous celebrity writes a song for you and he says your name right there in front of thousands of people.

I fell asleep without dreaming.

But around dawn I woke up again and I saw the T-shirt that covered up the TV screen and I thought, "Maybe I should pay attention to Ben now." So I got up and yanked it away. "Go ahead," I said to the monitor, "reveal all, I don't care anymore."

I expected to find a full description of everything that had happened in the last twenty-four hours: the concern, the escapade in the ventilation system, everything.

But instead, the computer message was:

LITTLE BROTHER, BY NOW THE MAN FROM THE WEBB FOUNDATION MUST REALLY BE BOTHERING YOU, AND YOU'VE PROBABLY BEEN SUCKERED INTO HIS LITTLE SCHEME ALREADY. I'M SURE HE'S TOLD YOU WHEN THE NEXT BIG PSYCHIC GET-TOGETHER TO PREDICT THE FUTURE IS. PRETTY NICE LAB HE HAS, HUH? ALL THOSE GADGETS—

"Wait a minute!" I said to myself. "That's not what happened at all . . . I didn't go down to the Webb Foundation. The man hasn't suckered me in . . ."

The whole message was like that. Way off. Nothing like the truth. "So you can be wrong!" I said. "You don't know everything. There's no magic. You predicted and planned and programmed and timed it in advance . . . but you didn't predict Zombie . . . you didn't predict the concert . . . didn't predict that I could stand up to the man from the Webb Foundation."

I started jumping up and down for joy and whooping. Aunt Casey came in in her nightgown, rubbing her eyes. I just pointed at the screen and babbled. I must not have made any sense. She went out and came back in with a tray of food.

"Eat," she said. "Then you'll talk slower."

"I can't, I'm too excited—"

But I did manage to gulp down a few slices of raw fish and swallows of hot tea. She watched me the whole time, with a broad grin on her face. "You have learned something important?" she asked me at last.

"The messages from the dead—whatever they are —they don't always know everything—I thought there was only one direction to go, one path. But suddenly I know there's hundreds of ways to go, hundreds and hundreds of futures to choose from, and I can find my own way, without any messages or magic symbols."

"Yes," she said. "To tell the future is not science, but art. To talk to spirits is not by a machine, but by feeling, out of the human heart."

"Can we have a séance, Aunt Casey? Can we call my brother back from the dead so he can answer all my questions?"

"What are your questions?"

"I want to know why he killed himself," I said.

"Poor boy. Do you really believe in spirits? Even I do not always believe it, though spirits pay for my mortgage. Maybe all you will hear is the echo of your own mind. And you do not need me for that."

"I need someone who will ferry me across the river and stay beside me to make sure I get home safely."

She nodded very solemnly and said, "Are you still afraid?"

"Of course I am, Aunt Casey," I said, hugging her and feeling how frail she was beneath her cotton sleeping kimono. "But I think I'm ready to face whatever's in the Forgetting Place."

I realized I was going to go back to Kansas after all. I had unfinished business with Benjamin Bhakti Madigan, but I was going to finish it on my own terms.

CHAPTER 19

Crossing the River

THIS IS what going back to McDougal, Kansas, was like:

I knew now that I really wanted to go home. But I couldn't bring myself to call right away. I have a lot of pride. I think I have too much sometimes. Instead, I called Mr. Miles's store and told him I was ready to come back soon. He agreed to keep it a secret. I told him I wanted to make it a surprise, but to tell you the truth, it was just that I was scared to just come barging in like nothing had happened. I remembered how jealous I'd felt when Sissy Pavlat had answered the phone that day, how she'd seemed so much at home there. Did I really belong with all those people, after everything I had seen? I wanted to be part of them again. But I was so totally afraid of how they would see me and how I would see them. When your eyes have been opened, it's hard to close them again.

I did see Zombie the next day. If this weren't real life, if it were just one of those soap operas . . . I would probably be telling you that after her confrontation with the Big Truth she changed completely and learned the meaning of life and straightened out and gave up drugs and gave up all those terrible things she had been doing to punish her family and herself. But I can't tell you that, because life's not the same as television no matter how much they try to sell you on the illusion that it is.

We met and we talked—about other things. I told her a lot about Ben and she told me about her dad, although I don't know if it was stuff she remembered or stuff she made up. It's going to be a long time before she can separate out reality from fantasy. I don't know whether or not I love her. I guess I'll find out eventually.

We met the day after that, too, and played video games together down at Guru Jack's Nirvana Games Unlimited. That evening I stayed over at her house. After you get past the groupies at the gates and all the security guards, you arrive at a perfectly normal kind of a house. It looks like it could have been plucked out of Kansas (by a tornado, maybe?) and set down on the grounds of Tygh Simpson's estate.

The only thing that is really unusual about their house is that they have a humongous old wooden roller coaster in their backyard. And that evening, instead of talking, we just rode it, over and over, against the setting sun. The wind roared and we screamed and we felt our pain and anger melt into the air. After that we sat in this totally gigantic spa for a while and Tygh came and sat with us.

I didn't feel like totally overawed in the presence of my greatest idol anymore. But, you know, what I did feel was something far more important. It was like we had both gone through a terrifying journey together and we had seen sights and fought monsters together —well, maybe *I'd* been the one fighting the monster alone, in the end, but I couldn't go on being mad at him for his moment of weakness. We shared something that no one else could ever share. It was something like what brothers feel. It wasn't that Tygh took Ben's place, you understand. But I knew now that even the worst wounds can be healed, and I had hope. Friends aren't brothers, but Tygh was like something in between.

Late at night he went down to the studio or something, and Zombie and I watched bad horror movies all night on the VCR and no messages from Ben popped up on the screen.

In the morning we had the strangest good-bye I have ever said to anyone. It was wordless and quick. She vanished quickly into the house. It seemed like so mundane somehow, just stepping into the car and being driven back to Burbank. I thought of a million things to say as I leaned back in the seat, watching a videotape of the concert on the car TV, seeing the two of us riding the cloud down to the bank of the river. Maybe I wouldn't ever see her again. Kansas seemed like a whole 'nother universe.

Aunt Casey shut the house down, and Guru Jack, she, and I piled into her gurumobile and went east.

I slept most of the journey. I guess I was worn out from everything that had happened. Now and then I dreamed of Ben. They were not the same dreams that had haunted me before. They were more like memories. Things that had slipped my mind for so long. Perhaps I was retrieving them from the Forgetting Place.

I remembered, many years ago, trying to teach him how to pitch. The ball glided upward and then plopped into the river. "You'll always be a klutz," I said. "You'll always be a dumb jock," he said, laughing. I was maybe nine. I remembered him building his first spaceship out of an old trash can. Or was it a robot? It was long before Stephanie was born.

The desert rolled by. Later there were mountains, and a mist hung over the road. All the way home, I clutched the Jiffy Bag with Ben's gifts and clues to my chest as if it were a teddy bear.

More and more bits and pieces of the past . . . the Forgetting Place was yielding up old treasures. But the one thing, the dark thing that lay hidden there, I still could not discover. I never saw Ben during the journey. There wasn't any magic. The ghost—real or imagined—didn't appear at all. I knew it was waiting for me at home.

After two days we reached McDougal. It was Saturday. It was, as a matter of fact, the day that the Webb Foundation's big telepathic marathon was supposed to take place. Midnight, yeah. Of course, that would be one in the morning in McDougal. It was a disturbing fact and I flicked it aside, but it kept coming back to bother me.

The sun was setting as we left Route 50. The road toward my house was half buried with leaves. The smell of home, the smell of rich earth and moist leaves, the smell of the river . . . I couldn't believe I'd lived without those things for so long.

We passed Mr. Miles's store. There was a light on inside, and I wondered if he was sitting there waiting for me to come back. At the turn before my house I suddenly cried out, "Stop, stop, please stop."

Guru Jack pulled up under a great big evergreen. "What is it you are wanting? A few words of wisdom before the great confrontation, isn't it?"

"Jack, give the boy a break," Aunt Casey said softly.

"It's okay," I said. "I'm not afraid of going back

anymore. But like there's something I've got to do first. Can we get back onto Route 50 and go east a little ways?"

"Yes," Aunt Casey said. "I hope that the cemetery is still open this late."

She really could read minds, my Aunt Casey.

We turned around. We went back to the highway. I could see the cottonwoods of Starry Havens, spindly and black in the twilight. We had to make about a ten-mile detour, though, to the bridge, to reach it. When we reached the bridge, it was totally wrapped in mist. Like the dream. Like the scene at the rock concert. I felt aching cold seep into me.

"We can go back if you want," Aunt Casey said, but from the way she said it I knew she knew I wasn't going to.

"Strange," I said. "In the dream it was always a boat, not a car."

"Well, we are living in the twentieth century, you know," Jack said. "We are not being obliged to travel by medieval conveyances."

We were across before he had finished his sentence. In the dream it had been an agonizing crossing . . . with the riverbank receding farther and farther . . . always out of reach. This way I didn't have time to brood over the consequences.

Jack stopped the car. The gateway to Starry Havens was all twisted bars of iron just like in a horror movie. There was fog everywhere. Beyond it were rows of gravestones. The cottonwoods stood by the river, and I could hear the water murmuring.

The three of us got out. I tried the gate. But it was padlocked. I looked at them, thinking, "They've got to know some way out of this." They didn't say anything at first, but just watched me shaking the gates and trying to pry the padlock apart with my hands. I stopped and looked at them. They were both dressed in "civilian" clothes—"Don't want to be scaring the natives," Guru Jack had told me—Aunt Casey in a flimsy summer dress and a woolen shawl, the guru in a denim jacket and frayed cords and one of those wide, flowery ties they used to wear in the olden hippie days. "What'll I do?" I said at last.

"You'll have to squeeze through the bars," Aunt Casey said. "That means we can't come with you."

"But—" I felt wild panic suddenly. "You have to be there with me! I can't face him alone! You're the one who knows how to summon up the spirit guide, Aunt Casey, and how to do the voices of the dead—"

"You didn't do so badly yourself," she said, reminding me of the time I had seemed to be Zombie's dead father.

I turned to Jack. "You've got to come," I said. "If I get sucked in too deep, you can pull me out with one of your jokes or you can start talking about science fiction maybe."

Jack said, "Science fiction? Not this time, J.J." I knew he was being serious, because he wasn't laying on his big Indian accent shtick.

"Do you remember when you slithered through the theater's ventilation system to save Zombie's life?" Aunt Casey said. "You were the only one who could do it. Only a scrawny adolescent like you. It was almost as if the ventilation shaft were designed so that only you could make your way through the maze."

"You're saying that it's all fate, or something?"

"No," they both said at the same time.

Aunt Casey said, "You don't need us. You don't need magic tricks. You don't need illusions. What you have to do is for you alone to do. I've taught you all I know."

"But who will speak in the voice of—"

"Your heart will speak for you, not the lips of an old quack like me."

I couldn't wait around any longer. You see, the way I had seen it, we would have one of those séances and I'd have all the pain washed away from me. I'd seen it happen when Zottoli burst into tears, hearing his old friend's voice. Zombie had had some kind of release when she thought she was talking to her dad, even though she thought he was telling her to walk away from life.

So I turned sideways and eased myself into the graveyard. The metal was wet and its touch made me shiver. I was totally terrified. But I saw that they were still standing there, in front of the gurumobile, encouraging me, so I took heart. I yanked the trusty Jiffy Bag through, and walked on. I knew roughly where Ben's grave would be, because, of course, I had watched the funeral from across the river.

I looked back after about two minutes and they weren't there anymore. The car was gone too. Grimly I told myself, "Maybe they're walking out on me, but I'm going to finish what I set out to do."

I waited. There was nothing to hear except the whisper of the river. The mist gathered. There was no more sun. A pale half-moon shone. The headstones cast long shadows and kind of zebra-striped the paved pathway. "Ben?" I said. "Are you there?"

Maybe I heard something. Just the leaves rustling. Quickly I walked toward it, knowing that if I slowed down I might panic and run away. There was a new headstone right by the edge of the water. Between the tree trunks I could see water and more mist. The headstone read:

BENJAMIN BHAKTI MADIGAN
1970–1987

That's all. Nothing about how he used to dream wild dreams. Or about his computer programs or his fascination with exotic facts or his maybe occult powers. "How could they do this to you?" I said aloud.

"Why not?" Was that a voice I had heard? I whirled around and saw only shadows. But maybe . . . there in the trees . . . a face? Leaning against one of the headstones . . . an elbow, a curled lip, a smile? I tried to stare harder but the more I stared, the less I could see.

I said, "I don't know if this is magic like Aunt Casey's magic or if it's all in my mind. If I'm crazy, I guess I'm crazy."

"Hey, little dude," said the voice. Ben's voice. I knew it as well as my own. Like he was standing right beside me, only if I turned around to touch him he was gone. "I see you came to join me after all. You always do what I do, don't you? Even to the bitter end."

I said, "I told you already. I'm not going to kill myself. I didn't come here to join you in death . . . I came to say good-bye."

"Good-bye? What do you mean, good-bye? I'm your brother, damn it! Your big hero, the one who always knows all the answers."

The shadow flickered. For a moment his face seemed completely clear. He was kind of pouting, the way he always did when he wanted me to do something I was reluctant to do . . . like be a guinea pig in one of his experiments.

"Ben—" I said. The face vanished. I couldn't look at him directly at all.

"Listen, little dude." The voice was behind me somewhere. "You want to find out why I did it, don't you? That's why you ran away from home, that's why you got into all that heavy occult spiritualism stuff. Nothing satisfied you, so now you've come for the straight dope. I guess those messages from beyond the grave got to you too."

I said, "There was nothing in those messages that you couldn't have figured out before you . . ."

"Died! Say it! Died, died, died!"

"Shut up!" It occurred to me how much I'd always resented him speaking my words for me, butting into my life and taking over. I felt totally guilty for thinking those thoughts, but I had to go on. "Everything you said was ambiguous. Of course you knew I'd run away. After all those clues you planted. You know me well, Ben, and you've been observing me all my life, I know that. I'm not denying it. But there was nothing supernatural in the messages. You could have programmed them all beforehand, to be delivered by modem, once a day. And when something happened that you had absolutely no way of knowing about . . . when Zombie appeared in my life . . . your messages really started to miss their target."

"Zombie . . . the walking dead."

"I saved her, Ben. That was important, you know. I stopped her from following you, throwing away everything."

"Do you know what you saved her from?" Ben's voice was cold, sneering. I'd never heard him sound like this when he was alive, even when we were quarreling. "Shut your eyes and I'll show you. There's a dark spot inside your mind. All the things you never want to face are there. But I wanted to face those things. I wanted to know things. I wanted to know the future. Close your eyes and I'll show you what I saw . . . it should be easy. All the big psychics are concentrating today . . . the future is in the air, ready to be plucked down . . . like a ripe fruit. Do it, Jeremi-

ah Johnson, do it." I couldn't help myself. I reached
out with my mind. Everything went black, but at the
center of the blackness there was a circle of even
greater blackness. "Go on," Ben said, "go inside."

Suddenly I heard Zombie's voice too: "You try to
see what's going to happen, sometimes you seem to
see it like so clearly, and you see there's no place to go
anymore."

Then like all these alien images started streaming
through my mind. Something had seized control of
me and I wasn't seeing with my own eyes anymore
... and what I saw was horrifying. I saw cities
exploding and people being killed. I saw thousands of
Rambo clones charging down hillsides with their
M-16s blasting and blowing people away. The sky was
red. The fields were on fire. A skyscraper splitting
down the middle and the people spilling out over the
city. It was all horrifying but it didn't seem real to
me. It was too much to understand all at once. I
gasped. "Is this what you saw? Is this the future?"

"Yeah." Ben's voice was ugly. "That's why I bailed
out."

"But you don't know that it's the future. You told
me yourself that there may be millions upon millions
of possible futures, and that maybe we could see into
other universes. Maybe it's some other universe's
future you saw. I mean, you can't know for sure. Life
means not knowing."

"Oh, give up, little brother. The world is doomed. I
saw it, now you've seen it. Stop going around saving
people's lives. It's all senseless."

"I can't believe you're saying this to me, Ben!"

"I'm saying it. I want you to die."

I paused. The vision was already dissolving. I only
half remembered it. It was like a random picture that
flashes by when you're clicking through the channels

on cable. "You killed yourself because of that tiny glimpse into—"

"You got it."

But I couldn't believe his answer. Maybe it was true that Ben had had a vision like that. But he must have been slipping out of the real world long before that. Slowly it dawned on me that my brother might have been insane . . . might have slowly been going crazy, for years, even . . . and nobody had noticed. Because he was B.B. Madigan, boy genius, and you just took it for granted that he'd be weird . . . I was shivering like crazy now.

The voice went on. Sometimes I could see his face and sometimes I could only see the moonlight on the gravestones. "I'm in the Forgetting Place now. I never have to see those visions again. Do you understand? I'm free."

"Free! What a joke."

"You could have set that girl free, too, but instead you forced her to go on living."

"Don't you dare tell me that helping Zombie was a bad thing!" I shouted. In the silence, an owl hooted. I was too angry to be scared.

"You can make up for your mistake, J.J.," Ben said. "Look. So easy. Put your hand on the headstone."

I reached out to touch the marble. Suddenly I was clutching something cold . . . cold and clammy . . . a pistol! I stared at my hand but I could see nothing. "More illusions!" I shouted.

"The world is a terrible place. Get out while you can."

"Well, maybe it is. But I'm better off sticking around to dream I can make it better. I'm better off with hope. You don't know everything anymore, Ben. I've seen things you've never seen. You're wrong this time, Ben, because I've learned something you never learned. I know that life is better than death. No matter what."

"That's just your childish self speaking, kiddo! Grow up! Join the grown-ups, the ones who've walked away, the ones on the other side of the river!"

Softly I said, "I was with someone who felt the way you did. Her world was way worse than yours. But if you'd seen her at the moment that she pulled back from the brink of suicide, you'd know that you can't give up hope, you can't give up dreaming."

"Don't you want to be perfectly like me?" There was a whining quality in his voice and he sounded like a spoiled little boy who isn't getting his own way. . . . "You always wanted to be just like me. Now you can be."

And I realized that this wasn't true anymore. Being separated from Ben had forced me to become myself. I wasn't a part of him anymore, I wasn't my brother's shadow.

"No," I said firmly. "You can't really be telling me to kill myself. My brother would never want me to die. And if you're trying to make me die, *you're not really my brother.*" And when I had said those words, I knew at last that they were true.

"But . . ." Ben's voice quavered. When he spoke again, it had lost its harshness and it sounded so much like how I remembered him that I almost took back what I'd said. "I miss you. I want you to be with me. Wash away all your pain, J.J. Step into the Forgetting Place and be with me forever."

"You're not my brother," I said again, turning my back on the gravestone. "There are two Bens, you know. The Ben I loved and hero-worshiped . . . the Ben who cleverly programmed all those messages into the computer and left those fiendish clues for me to analyze . . . he's gone. I know that now. But because I hated losing him, because I wanted to hold on to him, I built another Ben in my mind. I made him up out of my favorite memories. I saw him in daydreams and nightmares. And when the messages from my dead brother arrived, I started thinking that this Ben I created had like somehow come to life. But it's not true, is it? It's like the images Aunt Casey creates for her clients. The people who come to her need those images, and for them, they're pretty real, I guess.

"There's a lot of me in the Ben I created. Because I wanted so much to hold on, I thought that Ben would want to hold on to me just as much. The Ben I created wanted me to be like him . . . to be with him . . . to be dead. But that's not how the real Ben would be. My brother loved me. He didn't want me dead. Go away now. You're not my brother and you never will be. Go back into the dark part of me. Where you came from. Where you belong."

I stopped. I was crying so hard it blurred the moon and the pale tombstones. I just knew he was going to say something terrible to hurt my feelings, to open up all my wounds again. But I didn't care. I just stood there crying my heart out like a little kid.

Gradually I realized he wasn't going to say anything more. I dried my eyes on my T-shirt. The leaves rustled and the shadows shifted. But there were no ghosts. They were leaves and shadows, nothing more.

"Ben?" I said very gently.

I strained to hear. But there was only the wind and the river. At that moment I knew that I would never see Ben again or hear his voice. I didn't know grief could be like this. It was appalling to feel this empty. But behind the loss there was a sense of freedom too. I mean, I felt free to cry, free to seek to be strong again, free to hope.

"Good-bye, Ben," I said.

He was gone.

I'd been angry with him for dying: I knew that now. I'd resented him so much—I'd hated him for abandoning me. But now I also knew how much I loved him and how much I will always love him. I knew him better than I'd known him when he was alive, because now I knew he had never been perfect. But it didn't matter anymore because the Ben I loved and still love is the real Ben and not an idea, a shadow, an imagined thing.

I ached because I wanted to touch him so badly. Instead I stood there hugging the chill empty air hard to my chest.

CHAPTER 20

Coming Home

I WENT BACK to the gate. Guru Jack and Aunt Casey and the car were still missing. What time was it? Maybe they'd gone to find food or something.

I went back to Ben's grave. The wind was stronger now and the mist almost all gone. I touched the headstone. I felt no magic. Then I heard voices coming from far away, across the rippling of the water.

I slipped through the line of cottonwoods to the bank. I could see our house. And the shack. There were lights on in the house. I could see them glinting from behind the woods. I could barely make out the voices. There was the singsong of Guru Jack and Aunt Casey's calm, deliberate voice. And others too, others I hadn't heard in so long . . . had it been that long? I realized that it had only been a couple of weeks since I decided to walk away from Ben's funeral. But it seemed like another age.

I took my shoes off and stepped into the water. I felt the mud of the riverbank ooze between my toes. It was a totally familiar sensation that I'd known since I was a little kid. The riverbed was squishy but my feet remembered exactly where to tread. I knew every cranny, every jag, every smooth stone.

The water was cold but I waded farther out. I held the Jiffy Bag over my head so it wouldn't get splashed. When I came back out by the shack, I was sopping wet and freezing. Quickly I put my sneakers back on and made my way back down the path through the woods. Mom and Dad were standing in the backyard. They were waiting for me. They were dressed in a strangely formal way—Dad wore a jacket and the tie with the bookstore logo on it, and Mom wore a faded party dress. As if this were some special ceremony and they felt they had to dress up somehow. Because I had come home. I was moved by that. They didn't say anything to me for a long time, and I didn't go up to them. I just looked from one to the other, feeling a little awkward. Dad was rubbing his beard and Mom was folding and unfolding her hands.

After a bit I realized that they felt just as awkward as I did. So I smiled a little. My mom began to cry.

"I—" Dad and I began at the same time.

"No, go ahead, son."

"No, Dad, you talk."

We both shrugged. Dad stared at the moon, then at his feet.

Mom said, "I'm so terribly sorry. I guess we forgot all about you . . . we forgot to include you in our grief. We didn't mean to fight over chickens. We didn't mean to fight at all, but . . . we were badly hurt, you know. Are you ashamed of us? Forgive us, J.J."

"Forgive?" I said softly. "Ashamed?"

"We do love you, you know," my father said.

"I know that now," I said. "How can you ask me to forgive you? It's me who should be asking you. I wanted to hold on to my grief so much. I didn't want anyone else to have any. Like a little kid with a candy bar."

"Remember how you used to try to make him play baseball?" Dad said.

"Yeah." I suddenly laughed out loud, remembering him fumbling and shambling around the yard.

"I bet you never knew that he and I practiced secretly a couple of times, because he didn't want to look too much like a klutz in front of you."

"What?" Another new idea.

"He always wanted to be like you, you know," Mom said. "He adored you. He was caught up in his intellectual world, but sometimes he felt he was living through you—"

"No," I said, "it's me who wanted to be like him—"

Oh, God, it hurt. It still hurts, sometimes.

We talked for a long time about the past. After a while it didn't seem to hurt so much, because there were so many good times to remember. All this while I never moved any closer to my parents and they never came close to me. They were keeping their distance, like maybe I was an escaped tiger from the circus or something like that. We were wary of each other. I guess I was afraid this gentle moment we were sharing would go away, would be shattered by some dumb argument. And they were scared I'd lose my temper and up and run back to Burbank.

"Is there any food?" I said at last.

My mom laughed, a bit embarrassed. Then she said, "Sure, honey. In the house."

We walked slowly in through the back door. The kitchen was full of people . . . Jack, holding Stephanie in his arms and bouncing her up and down, Aunt Casey already making herself at home by the stove, cooking up a storm.

Mom looked at Aunt Casey in an odd sort of way. I got the impression that she'd somehow never approved of her. She was about to say something —something catty, I guessed—but stopped herself short. Then she smiled, trying to make peace. It seemed that there was a lot going on in my family that had passed right over me.

The next moment Sissy Pavlat came breezing through. She just said, "Hi, J.J. Did you bring me any cool shades from L.A.?" She'd filled out a bit. Unless she'd taking to stuffing socks into the front of her sweater. She was using perfume, too—a scent I'd never smelled in Kansas. Amazing.

Before I could answer her, Mr. Miles popped in from the living room. He saw me and said, "I see the tornado brought you home again, kid."

"I guess."

"Candy?"

"No, I think I'll settle for one of Aunt Casey's holistic concoctions."

Mr. Miles shrugged. "A couple weeks in California and he thinks he's above us country folks!" he said. It took me a second to realize he was joking. Then we all laughed.

"Jack! You son of a—" Mr. Miles began. "I didn't realize you'd turned into a dothead! You sure look different from when the two of us were panhandling tourists on Haight-Ashbury. . . ."

"Come off it," said Guru Jack. "References to my checkered past are being very bad for my image, isn't it? What if I were to tell them that you used to have hair down to your derrière and a peace sign tattooed on your—"

"What?" I said, startled out of my mind. "You mean you used to be a hippie too, Mr. Miles?"

"How do you think I know all these people?" he said.

Like, I was totally staggered by this revelation. But

before I had time to faint, Stephanie said, "J.J."

Everyone stopped and stared at the baby. She gurgled and coughed up some gross gooey stuff.

"Wait a minute," I said. "Stephanie can't talk, can she?"

"She can now," Dad said. "Amazing. She said 'Da-da.' Just goes to show who's boss around here."

"She did not! She distinctly said 'J.J.'!"

"Come on," Mom said. "Obviously what she said was "Ma-ma." Babies always say that first."

"J.J.," the baby said again, staring straight at me.

I took Stephanie from Guru Jack's arms and rocked her back and forth, back and forth. She smelled of baby powder. Her eyes were like Ben's eyes: wide-open, serious, questioning. Babies are not like teddy bears; they move around a lot and you're always scared they're going to like make a mess on your shirt or something. But I didn't care. Let Mom and Dad think whatever they wanted. I knew what the baby had said. And I thought, "I'm your biggest brother now, kid. And no way am I going to walk out on you, no way, never." She started to giggle. Maybe she could read my mind.

My family—not just Mom and Dad and Stephanie, but all of them—stood all around me. There was a long silence. I wondered if I was supposed to like reveal the meaning of life or something. You know, the Big Truth that everyone's supposed to be searching for. I didn't say anything.

But I was thinking. I took the composite tarot card out of the Jiffy Bag. It was kind of soggy. I put it on the kitchen table and everyone crowded around it like it was some kind of magical device. Death . . . transformation. Two sides of the same thing. Did Ben think he was going to change the world by dying? I knew that at least one person had been transformed. Me.

And because of that transformation, I was able to say, with a straight face, without forcing myself, without being icky cute or sentimental, to my parents: "I want you to know, you guys, that I really, really love you. I love you. I'm alive and I'm home and I love you."

I think I released something in my parents then. Maybe it was something from their old hippie days that they weren't comfortable with anymore, so they locked it up and threw away the key. But they'd been fumbling for the key all these years. That was the reason for the psychobabble and those big fights over nothing. When you're a kid, you think your parents are all-powerful and know everything. But now I know they're struggling too. We're struggling together, them and me. That makes us more alike. That makes me not a kid anymore, I guess. Well, some of the time anyways.

Because I thought my parents were like these superbeings, I thought they were going to be like the ferryman in the story of that Japanese Noh play and they were going to row me across the river and teach me how to conquer my pain. But now I could see that maybe I had to be their ferryman too. And lead them away from their own Forgetting Place.

What happened next was that I was still holding the baby but I clumsily tried to put my arms around Mom too, and then Dad kind of joined in and I think maybe the others were in on it too. We were hugging each other so tight, sharing all the things we felt.

I don't know if it was grief or joy. I guess I was hurt and happy all at once. It was like one thing, one big, overwhelming emotion.

*   *   *

I talked to Zombie on the phone the other day. I'm going to go back to L.A. next summer and visit with all my new friends. Tygh is making a music video of that new song of his, "Crossing the River." He wants to keep that part about me and Zombie floating down from heaven on a cloud, except it will be all special effects. Matte photography, I think. I saw it in Universal Studios that time I took the tour with Guru Jack. It's how they make Superman fly.

He wants all of us to be in it—Zombie and me and Mom and Dad and Guru Jack and Aunt Casey and even Mr. Miles. We all have to join some kind of union so we can be in it—weird legal stuff.

It'll be awesome to see us all on MTV. They'll make us up so we look totally perfect. My friends are all going to wet themselves with envy, I can just see it.

It's a beautiful song and I think the images will be beautiful too, and it will ring true to a lot of people.

But no matter how beautiful we look, it won't be like what really happened. Because a TV screen can't show what was in our minds. It can only show what's on the surface of things.

I'm part of the real world, and I can tell reality from illusion.

But I've learned that they can both be the truth.

About the Author:
Somtow Papinian Sucharitkul (S. P. Somtow) was born in 1952 in Bangkok. He grew up in Europe, was educated at Eton and Cambridge, and came to America about ten years ago. His first career was as a composer, and his works have been performed all over the world. While working in the field of music he was appointed Thai Representative to the International Music Council of UNESCO, and conducted various orchestras in Europe and Asia.

In 1979 his first science-fiction stories started to appear. He won the 1981 John W. Campbell Award for best new writer as well as the Locus Award for his first novel, *Starship & Haiku*. Two of his short stories have been nominated for the prestigious Hugo Award. His science-fiction books, written as Somtow Sucharitkul, include the *Inquestor* series and the satirical *Mallworld*.

Recently he has branched out into other fields, writing as S. P. Somtow. His new works include a horror novel, *Vampire Junction*, and a historical fantasy, *The Shattered Horse*, which won the 1986 Daedalus Award. He has also written animated cartoon scripts, book reviews for the Washington *Post* and the Cleveland *Plain Dealer*, and has a monthly column of film criticism in *Fantasy Review*.

Forgetting Places is his second book for young adults. His first was *The Fallen Country*.

He lives in Los Angeles.